Murder, by the Book

Murder, by the Book

Stephen Budiansky

Black Sheep Press

ISBN 143483767X

Printed in the United States of America

To Richard and Mary

Gather ye rosebuds while ye may,
Old Time is still a-flying,
And this same flower that smiles today
Tomorrow will be dying.
    —Robert Herrick
    To the Virgins to Make Much of Time

Violence is the repartee of the illiterate.
    —Alan Brien

Cauliflower is cabbage with a college education.
    —Mark Twain

✤ 1.

Ted Gilpin shifted uneasily in his chair and, for the fifth time, glanced down at the note he had written himself before the meeting.

"Sit down and shut up," it read.

No one else in the room showed any inclination to challenge the speaker. In fact, the other faculty members sitting around the dingy metal table looked mostly just bored. Maybe they were better actors than he was, Gilpin thought. Or maybe they had been gassed into a state of passive docility by the miasma of corporate jargon that had enveloped every phrase that had been wafting over them for the last half hour.

Gilpin scrawled a note on his pad and surreptitiously slid it over to Eric Travis on his left. "Did he just say we're going to <u>sell</u> naming rights to individual courses????"

Travis raised his eyebrows in a facetious expression of mock-horror, vigorously pointed to Gilpin's "Sit down and shut up" message, and resumed his poker face.

By the looks of him, Vice President for Marketing and Finance Bob "Juice" Welch appeared to have taken an unaccountable wrong turn on his way to introduce the Rotary Club's Citizen of the Year Award before a group of fellow back-slapping golf players at the ballroom of the local Marriott. He wore a loudly striped vivid blue shirt with a contrasting, rounded solid-white collar; a gold tie tack; large square gold cufflinks on his French cuffs; a sort of silvery tie; a very expensive looking watch; dark suit; and brown, elaborately tooled wingtips. A small invisible cloud of cologne hovered over him. His silver hair was immaculately shaped.

The academics wore blue jeans, zippered fleece pull-overs, and Reeboks. The conference room, located on the third floor of Trojan Hall, the creaking pseudo-Gothic humanities building, favored the academics. A note of indeterminate vintage stuck to the dusty fluorescent fixture over the table stated REPLACE THIS BULB, a tangle of computer cables and power strips sprawled on the floor, and a roll of toilet tissue perched atop an abandoned filing cabinet in the corner, bereft of its drawers. A blackboard that hadn't been used for years occupied the far wall. An analog clock on the facing wall was running ten minutes slow. Welch seemed as unfazed by his audience and surroundings as they were of him.

"So at the end of the day," he continued, "we need to ask whether we are driving our customer-centric education solutions to the next level. The 21st century university must competitively address the demands of what I call the *merging* marketplace of ideas and business. That means both monitizing the assets we have, and leveraging the new ideas that will keep us competitive in the future."

He paused with practiced effect. "If we don't, we're—as I like to say—circling the drain." Like all habitual users of business clichés, the Vice President delivered this mot with a small self-satisfied chuckle and the air of someone who had just invented it himself.

An uncomfortable silence filled the room, accentuated by the steady drone of leaf blowers from the platoon of grounds workers placidly rearranging leaves in the quadrangle below.

"I've wanted to have these informal meetings with small groups of faculty," Welch smoothly continued into the vacuum, "as part of our university-wide Innovation Initiative. Feedback is an integral component of the process. Unless we involve all of our customer bases—and that includes your faculty, your students, your parents, your local business community—the university will continue to slip in the critical area of thought leadership."

Another long pause. Everyone was studiously avoiding making eye contact with the speaker. Gilpin stared at his pad, Travis appeared fascinated by the clock, several others around the table seemed to have discovered an urgent need to penetrate the inner mysteries of the weaving pattern of their socks. Wendy Heatherton peered with great concentration into the small bag of fancy chocolates that she had been working her way assiduously through, though with no evident enjoyment, during the meeting.

Only Dr. John Doe, his open Midwestern face framed by oversized aviator glasses, looked eager to contribute.

"Ted? How about you—feedback?" Welch asked.

Gilpin cleared his throat. This was always happening to him. He envied Travis's serene ability to listen to endless bullshit with cynical tranquility. Hell, he envied Welch's idiot-savant ability to *deliver* endless bullshit with such polished political savvy. Here he had been struggling to keep his mouth shut for the last half hour, and now he was going to be forced to let his righteous indignation make a fool of himself once again.

What was worse was that he was in the right, dammit. He thought of the line spoken by one of the Oxford women dons in *Gaudy Night* to describe Lord Peter Wimsey: "That is a man able to subdue himself to his own ends." Why couldn't he ever "subdue himself"?

But then, Lord Peter's character was the projection of a highly literate—and sexually frustrated—woman novelist's idealization of early twentieth-century masculinity. It was ridiculous that he should feel inadequate comparing himself to a fictional character from a previous century. One of the occupational hazards of being an English professor, no doubt. The new editor of *Experiential Studies in Deconstruction* had just sent an email soliciting contributions that fused literary analysis with "the autobiographical memoir of the subconscious." Maybe there was a publishable paper in this. Gilpin's wandering thoughts were pulled up by the abrupt realization that everyone in the room was now looking at him. Feeling profoundly dissatisfied with himself, he sighed, and, resigning himself to the inevitable, plunged in.

"Er, Bob, did I understand you to say you're proposing to sell *naming* rights to courses?" He was already sounding shrill.

A smooth, plastic smile of recognition flashed across Welch's square face. "Absolutely, Ted. I'm glad you picked up on that point, Ted. It's just a logical extension of the branding initiative we launched earlier this year. It's a matter of what I call taking branding to the next level."

"But—never even mind the ethics of this for a minute—*how* can this possibly even *work?*"

"Well, Ted, it's really not rocket science. *Or* brain surgery." Welch again gave one of his self-satisfied chuckles. "Of course many in the university arena have been leveraging naming opportunities on professorships, buildings, quadrangles, sports facilities, parking garages, and so on for years. But in seeking input from the business community, we came to recognize that the customer base found these opportunities too static. They're looking for more dynamic ways to achieve the synergy and traction they're looking for. That of course is what was behind our very successful roll-out last year of partnering opportunities for certain activities that the student customer base relates to in a much more proactive way than just the strictly educational dimensions of the university."

He added, as if an afterthought, "Like, oh, the annual bonfire."

The casualness, as everyone in the room well knew, was an affectation, for the bonfire licensing deal had been one of Welch's great coups, written up in both *The Chronicle of Higher Education* and *Ad Age*. The annual freshman bonfire, which had been held the night before the last home football game every fall since the 1920s, was now officially the Freshman Jose Cuervo® Bonfire and Riot. It was part of a package deal that included an endowed chair in the School of Hospitality Management.

"And we're now seeking partners for more regular activities, too," Welch added. "I can tell you, in strict confidence for now of course, that we are in serious discussion with several interested partners for the naming rights to Tuesday."

"Tuesday?" Gilpin asked, his genuine bewilderment momentarily displacing the mounting sense of outrage he was feeling.

"Yes, I'm sure you know, Ted—if you're in touch with the student customer base—that the generic name for Tuesday here on campus is 'Boozeday.' But that obviously represents a grossly unopportunized naming opportunity."

Gilpin felt his head slightly swimming. "But, look, about the *courses.* Surely that's a completely different issue. I can't even imagine you're serious about this. This would be like..." He struggled for a metaphor that wouldn't seem precious or refined. Phrases involving "Philistines" and "moneychangers in the temple" popped into his mind but he quickly thought better of them. "Like running ads during a church service," he lamely concluded.

"Well, Ted, some of your more forward-looking religious denominations are out in front on that. But let me give you a specific example. Say you teach English, oh, 101."

"I don't."

"Well, Ted, let's *say* you do. Now, a logical synergy here would be to approach a member of our business community customer base that's interested in leveraging *English.* So we might—just as a hypothetical here—offer an opportunity to name that course, say Barnes & Noble English 101. Or Border's English 101. Or Kinko's English 101. You see the picture?"

"But—then what happens if you can't find a sponsor? I mean there are a lot courses that hardly are going to fit into some company's business plan, for God's sake."

"Well, Ted, this is the magic of the *merging* marketplace of ideas and business, as I mentioned. Not only will this be putting underutilized assets to work, but it is a way to ensure we're staying relevant to the needs of the 21st century."

"So you're saying that you're going to just *kill* any classes that can't get a business to sponsor them?" Gilpin was practically shouting now.

"Ted, this is *exactly* why feedback is so valuable. And I want you to know that I'm listening and I'm very grateful for your candid views."

"But...but...this is a violation of academic freedom!"

"Ted, I *respect* your strong feelings about this, and I assure you that we're always ready to listen."

Gilpin tried one final salvo. "But how is it serving the students to let a bunch of outside companies completely dictate what courses we will or will not offer?"

"Customers," the Vice President replied, his voice as level and unperturbed as always, just ever so slightly chiding now.

"What?"

"Ted, I'm sure you read my memo, but I know that old paradigms are sometimes hard to shift. I try to emphasize that we need to always refer to our students as *customers,* because that's what they in fact are. And as our mission statement says, our goal is to *delight* our customers and *exceed their expectations.* Now, Ted, I really think we need to move on here."

Travis gave Gilpin an "I told you so" look. From the end of the table, Wendy Heatherton launched into a long complaint about the university dog policy. He caught snatches of her Wellesley-inflected sneer going on about allergens and multiple chemical sensitivity disorder as he tried to calm himself down.

Gilpin glanced around the table and wondered again how his colleagues all remained so seemingly unconcerned. It could have been a Texas Hold'em tournament for all the emotion their faces betrayed. They were about twenty in all; several fellow members of the Department of Cognitive and Deconstructivist Studies—D-CADS for short—plus a mixed assortment of others from the humanities and sciences departments that occupied that end of the small campus.

As he looked around the room his eyes were arrested by an unfamiliar face. He had been aware of someone coming in late and taking a seat opposite him during his embarrassing colloquy with the Vice President, but had been too preoccupied to look over.

Now he couldn't stop looking. She was blond, with very soft-looking hair cut shoulder-length in a sort of shaggily athletic look. She was certainly beautiful, but it was an unusual kind of beauty—a longer and wavier nose and a straighter and more linear chin and jawline than most men would have found pretty, Gilpin thought. Yet there was something about those strong features that reminded him of a Renaissance artist's idealized vision of female beauty.

Was it Botticelli's *Young Woman in Mythological Guise* he was thinking of? He'd have to look it up.

Her skin was certainly straight from a Renaissance artist's canvas, opalescent and flawless. She was about Gilpin's age, he guessed, mid thirties. She had the unstudied ease in her clothes that only really beautiful women can pull off with such éclat— simple white T-shirt, jeans, long tan jacket of some sort of canvassy material, no jewelry. The only hint that there was anything studied in her appearance were the sunglasses perched with a kind of obviously affected casualness atop her head.

Gilpin suddenly realized that he had been staring for at least a minute at her breasts.

His eyes flicked up with a start and caught hers. They were piercing blue, tinged with just a hint of ironic amusement. It wasn't exactly the go-to-hell look he was used to seeing on beautiful women, but it wasn't exactly encouraging, either.

He looked away, his ears burning, and thought of all the papers he'd published about gender stereotyping and the objectification of women. Great, so he was an intellectual hypocrite as well as someone who couldn't keep his mouth shut at meetings.

He glanced over at Travis and saw he had the same amused

look in his eyes. Damn him, he always caught everything. Travis reached over, disengaged Gilpin's writing pad from his lap, wrote "Naughty naughty naughty," and handed it back.

Gilpin scowled and wrote on the next line, "Who is she?"

"WAY out of YOUR league," Travis wrote back. "Too smart."

"But who _is_ she?" Gilpin scribbled furiously, breaking his pencil point on the underline.

Tiring of the junior-high-school note passing, Travis leaned over and whispered into Gilpin's ear. "Anika de Groot. Physicist— does _quantum_ mechanics." Only Travis could say "quantum mechanics" and make it sound like a leer.

"I've been trying to get her interested in my interdisciplinary queer studies program, but no bites. Quite a dishy number, I'd say. Almost enough to make a fellow wish he were a lesbian."

Welch had finished subjecting the university dog policy to his standard armamentarium of business clichés and was making sounds indicating the meeting was about over when Anika suddenly spoke up. Her voice was a clear and melodious mezzo-soprano, the extra precision in her otherwise unaccented pronunciation the only indication that her native language was not English.

"Vice President." She said it quietly but with a self-assurance that caused all eyes in the room to turn to her at once.

"_Please_ call me Bob," Welch replied.

Anika showed no signs of having heard. "It is really most remarkable, Vice President," she began, "that we should have to read the student newspaper in order to learn that the university, at your apparent direction, is spending half a million dollars on a consultant's study for the development of a new name and logo for the university at a time when we cannot hire new faculty or even purchase urgently needed supplies of the most basic kind."

She then proceeded into a calm, perfectly organized, and merciless dissection of the Vice President, his management style, his budget priorities, the university's failure to recruit and promote women scientists, and the several hundred thousand dollars that had been lost as a result of his much-heralded campaign to make the university's operations more "businesslike" by outsourcing TA positions to graduate students at nearby colleges on a competitive-bidding basis. Even Welch seemed momentarily taken aback.

Gilpin found himself absurdly thinking of a Bach fugue—the blend of aching beauty and cool logic. God, she was magnificent, he thought. Self-possessed, rational, devastating. Everything he wasn't, he thought bitterly.

"If I can just take the first point first," Welch replied, quickly resummoning his synthetic poise, "then perhaps we can take some of your other points off-line, since they seem to be a little more department-specific. But the branding initiative you mention is an approved and vital component of our long-term strategic vision for keeping us in the world-class category as a learning institution. For example, our consultant has already given us some extremely valuable guidance on the renaming initiative. Their study has pointed out that all world-class universities have a one-word name, or at least nickname, and in my personal judgment I think that insight has already paid rich dividends for the investment we've made in this direction. Harvard—Brown—Penn—Caltech—MIT—all one word. And this is clearly the direction we need to follow if, at the end of the day, we're going to achieve our goals of excellence."

Gilpin gripped his writing pad for a few seconds. "MIT is *three* words," he finally blurted out.

Welch turned to him. "Yes, Ted, but it's written as one word. It's the look that carries the brand impact more than anything else."

Gilpin felt himself losing his temper again, all the worse be-cause he was aware Anika was now closely watching him. "But we already have a one-word nickname, for chrissake," Gilpin erupted. "Everyone has always called us 'Lawless'—back to the nineteenth century."

Welch visibly relaxed, clearly pleased to be sparring with a more manageable foe once again. "Yes, Ted, but that's *precisely* part of the whole program. Unbranding a negative impact is just as important as branding a positive impact. The law school as you can imagine has raised particular concerns on this point."

"And so just what has our great consultant come up with for our new one-word name that is going to magically make us 'excellent,' as you say?" Gilpin knew he was sounding like a petulant teenager but couldn't help it.

"This isn't final yet, of course, but I think we're definitely leaning toward 'The College Of.' It's got just that sort of edgy, hip, ironic, possibility-rich freshness that our customer base responds to."

"You're joking."

"Ted, everyone will have a definite opportunity to weigh in on this, I can absolutely reassure you, at the appropriate time."

"Anyway, isn't *that* three words?"

"Well, Ted, I'm sure I don't have to tell you, as an English expert, why 'The' and 'Of' don't count. I know you have some technical terminology for small words like that."

"You mean articles and prepositions?" The sneer that accompanied his words was, as usual, completely lost on Welch.

"Those are the ones, yup. Now, if you'll all excuse me, I have another meeting, but I *sincerely* appreciate all your input and feedback. I know we may have our differences, but we're all part of the same world-class team."

His final words were drowned by a scraping of metal chairs as the faculty members hastened for the door in the hopes of still beating the lunchtime rush at The Blue Olive, which dispensed inexpensive yet stupefying martinis, but did not take reservations.

Gilpin thought of going over to introduce himself to Anika but saw to his dismay that Travis had already buttonholed her and, from the snatches of phrases he caught across the room—"phallic symbolism of the electron," "esoteric theory as a metaphor for the closet," "relativity, quite a giveaway when you come to think of it"—he realized with a sinking heart that Travis had launched into a recital of his long theory that Einstein was gay.

Gilpin knew that Travis could hold on with relentless, bull-terrier-like grip for at least half an hour whenever he cornered an audience for this pet idea of his. He was good for ten solid minutes alone on his argument that $E=mc^2$ was a "gay equation," because of the way it flauntingly privileged variables over constants.

A gust of cologne intruded on his thoughts, and Gilpin realized Welch was touching him on the upper arm. "Ted, do you have a minute to walk back to my office with me?" the Vice President was saying. "There's something I'd like to take up off-line with you."

✛ 2.

The Evander Lawless College of North Ohio had its origins in a modest liberal arts institution founded by a fabulously successful small arms merchant and locally prominent patron of the arts.

In his dying years, wracked by guilt over the riches he had accumulated selling gunpowder and Minnié balls to both sides in the Civil War while assiduously avoiding military service himself, Evander Lawless had convinced himself that war itself could be made obsolete in the future if only everyone in their youth were required to study the plays of William Shakespeare, the music of Ludwig von Beethoven, the paintings of Michelangelo, and the poems of Robert Burns. He accordingly determined to give away all of his remaining riches in this cause.

The founding endowment to the college that would bear his name contained a stipulation in perpetuity requiring all students to devote at least half of their studies to these mandatory subjects. Succeeding generations of university administrators had been seeking to evade the requirement ever since.

Although the campus was small, Lawless's endowment had been more than sufficient to allow the university to keep up with the latest American collegiate architectural fashions over the years, and as Gilpin and Welch walked across the campus they passed the usual cacophony of building styles.

Next to the pseudo-Gothic towers of Trojan Hall loomed a vast Romanesque cathedral, still called Lawless Chapel and still home to an immense pipe organ, though it now hosted more Balinese gamelan concerts than Christian worship services. Across the street a stridently linear glass and steel 1970s Bauhaus science lab jostled with the obligatory titanium-sheathed Gehry building, its roof curving like the slopes of an extreme skiing course.

An ornately Victorian clapboard and shingle house, now used for official receptions, stood incongruously in the midst of it all; it was fronted by a wraparound porch filled with rocking chairs that gave the impression of a quaint summer resort that had seen better days, though the only view it offered the one or two students who were always occupying one of the chairs was of a series of large rusted steel plates and sheets of chain-link fence that formed a vast abstract sculpture completely filling the quadrangle in front.

A group of girls wearing heavy sweat pants and fleece jackets against the brisk October breeze were doing a kind of absurd dance around the sculpture while a boom box pounded out a metallic beat and a TA with a video camera recorded their efforts. A few male students with long sideburns or goatees and rings emerging in improbable spots from their faces stood around watching without much expression. A flock of posters advertising films, Yoga classes, a Dance Dance Revolution tournament, a "retro 90s rock concert," and a meeting of the Campus Crusade for Christ fluttered from kiosks.

Welch struck a brisk pace across the quadrangle as they walked silently side by side for several minutes, the combined roar of the leaf blowers and the dance music making conversation impossible. Gilpin tried to remember what he had read about the Vice President. He had graduated from Lawless in the early 1970s, having attended the college on a football scholarship and providing its perpetually losing team its solitary bright spot by setting a record one year as the top scoring place kicker in the Midwest Conference. He had majored in marketing and advertising and, upon graduating, was immediately hired by one of the big breakfast-cereal companies, whose chairman, Lawless Class of '62, always hired the top six Lawless athletes of each graduating class.

He had spent his entire career there, advancing steadily through the ranks and eventually reaching a high-level executive position. Last year he had taken early retirement and announced that he would return to his alma mater, at a drastic cut in pay, to "give something back" to the college that had done so much for him.

Gilpin and Welch crossed the street and followed the gravel path along the lagoon, a one-acre sump that a relentless flock of Canada geese was busily attempting to turn into something that was taking on the unmistakable characteristics of an open cesspool.

An interdisciplinary committee had been set up to find a humane solution to the problem, and their latest brainstorm had been to deploy a flotilla of decoys designed to look like dead geese, to scare away the live geese. But the film students who had made the decoys had gotten more and more carried away with the idea, and each week the decoys had become more and more macabre and Hitchcock-esque.

Gilpin noticed a new one he hadn't seen before, bobbing near the shoreline. It had a huge cleaver sticking out of its head and red splatters practically covering its body.

When there was at last no one near them, Welch spoke. "Ted, before I get to the main item I wanted to have a word with you about, let me just try to give you some clarity on the course issue. We see this definitely as a win–win for everyone. All I'm asking of *you* is to see if you can use your creative talents to touch all the bases. I just don't see why you have to go out of your way to—I'll be absolutely straight with you here one-on-one—*offend* the customer base with some of these course titles."

He pulled out a printed list from his briefcase and scanned down it. "I mean, really. Travis, 'Queering the Pitch: From "Eroica" to Erotica in Beethoven's Symphonies.' Glantz, 'Stupid Pet Tricks: Bestiality, Speciesism, and the Hidden Penetration of the "Other" in Shakespeare's Tragedies.' Heatherton, 'In the

Room the Women Come and Go, Talking of Fellatio: Women Speak Truth to the "Art" of Michelangelo.' Gilpin, 'Burns and Burns: From Robert to George: The Psychodynamics of Love and Humor.' Well, that one isn't too bad. But you get my point."

The cold air had swept away some of the dark clouds that had been dampening Gilpin's spirit from the meeting, and Welch's much more sincere-sounding approach now that they were alone kindled a small hope. "But, Bob, the whole reason the last administration brought us in and had us redo the core curriculum was to try to modernize what had become a huge intellectual embarrassment to the university."

"Ted, that's *exactly* why I sought to recognize the *unique* place that our core humanities scholars such as yourself play in the life of the university by creating the **D-CADS** department, which as you may, or may not know, is a first of its kind, something we're very proud of here. All I'm asking for is some flexibility. But now let me tell you why I wanted to speak to you." Welch stopped in the middle of the path. They were quite by themselves. "There's a little problem that's come up and I can't think of a better person to handle it."

"A better person than who?"

"You."

"Me?"

"Ted, it's just that sort of modesty that makes me know that I can count on you to be discreet. Now, it seems that Julie Glantz from your department hasn't been seen for several days and—"

"You mean she's been reported missing?"

"No, no, no. I'm sure it would be completely premature to say she's missing. There's probably some perfectly ordinary, simple explanation, and at a time when we're working so hard as a team to help redefine the image and brand of the college—we've got the *U.S. News* rankings coming up, after all—none of us want to make what I think would be a very serious error in judgment in overreacting."

"But when was she last seen?"

"Well, Ted, that's what we—the President and I—are hoping you'll be able to find out. She hasn't been to her classes for several days, which is not the level of service we like to project on the customer service front, as I'm sure I don't need to tell you, Ted. And my people tell me she's not at her home. And to be completely on the level here with you Ted, there have been some reports over the last few months of some well, erratic behaviors. I'll just leave it at that, since we do get into certain personnel and confidentiality issues very quickly here. But what we—the President and I—would like you to do is just talk to your colleagues—to Eric, and Wendy, and John, and Douad, and Mah-fukkah—"

"You mean Umfookah."

"Sorry, didn't catch that Ted?"

"Umfookah. That's how he pronounces it. It's spelled m-f-u-k-a but it's pronounced Umfookah. Accent on the second syllable."

"Right. Thanks Ted. I appreciate that. Anyway, as I was saying, you can just talk to them and see if they know anything about where she might have gone. It's probably one of those minor personal or professional crises that I know you academic and intellectual people sometimes have from time to time. A kind of occupational hazard. I understand that, and we just want to make sure everything is okay."

"But look, Bob, this is ridiculous. I mean I'm flattered by your confidence in me and all—"

"It's not just me, Ted. It's me *and* the President who have confidence in you."

"Yes, well, thank you very much. And thanks to the President. But I mean I'm not a detective. This is obviously something for the police."

Welch smiled with a look of admiration. "Ted, I said you were a modest man but I see that was an understatement. Now you can't deny that you know a thing or two about detectives. Why, I just saw it on the course list this morning as I was looking over it.

Last year you taught a whole course just on the detective novel. Let's see, where was it."

He scanned the list. "Here it is. 'Detective Fiction: Structure, Gender, and Theories.' There you have it." He smiled with the calm triumph of a man who had just proved his point beyond any possible further dispute.

Gilpin started to protest again, but Welch leaned in close to him, clasped his upper arm like a coach bucking up a young player, and said, "Ted, all we're asking is for you have a chat with your colleagues, take a look around her office, and let me—*us*— know what you find out. And if Julie's not turned up in another day or two, of course we'll just have to do what we have to do. But it would be a really significant contribution to the university if you'll take this on. I hope we can count on you. And Ted, we certainly won't forget how flexible you've been on this when we review how well your department is meeting the course-partnering goals."

Before he even realized it, Gilpin found himself having weakly given way to Welch's blandishments, and the Vice President was striding purposefully off down the path toward his next appointment.

Gilpin sat down on a bench on the tiny gravel beach and stared morosely for a while at the decoy with the hatchet in its head. Well, why not, he finally thought. It's not like there's any real detective work involved—and this business about his detective-novel class was nonsense either way. It wasn't as if detectives in real life went around tracing wayward heiresses or jewel-encrusted statuettes or jimmying locks like Philip Marlowe or lifting guns off of thugs like Sam Spade.

Or making brilliant deductions like Lord Peter Wimsey. That was just some soft soap from Welch. He obviously wants to try to hush things up, thought Gilpin, but it's perfectly natural that the first step before running to the police would be to ask her colleagues if they'd seen her or knew any reason she might have gone somewhere without letting anyone know. And it was also true enough that the notoriously flat-footed campus police would assuredly get hold of the wrong end of some idiotic idea once they jumped into it.

And then there was the fact that Julie Glantz had unquestionably been acting strange lately—Welch was dead right about that. No one knew what, if anything at all, she was working on these days. Over the last few months she had become oddly secretive about her research while simultaneously developing a genius for picking fights with everyone in the department. Most likely she had decided—or rather imagined—that she had been mortally insulted by someone or something and had gone off to sulk about it.

He began slowly ambling back to his office. God, how was it, he found himself wondering, that guys like Welch could make millions of dollars, talk anyone into anything, and not know an article from a preposition? Was education really that pointless?

The Welches of the world never seemed to have a moment's doubt about themselves, either. It wasn't just that they didn't know how little they knew—they didn't care, either. Maybe it all comes down to the fact that they were also the types who always effortlessly attracted beautiful women, Gilpin thought, and a sharp pang made him suddenly think of Anika de Groot.

Why didn't women ever seem to care how ignorant or phony these guys were, dammit. Why didn't the way they mangled the English language automatically disqualify them from any professions but digging ditches or flipping hamburgers, for that matter.

The slovenly dance troupe was still at it around the sculpture as Gilpin reached the quadrangle, the few goateed spectators having been replaced by a few subtly different goateed spectators, when he saw Anika and Travis walking ahead of him.

He hurried to catch up, but was still about thirty yards away when he saw her nod her head in a quick parting gesture to Travis and slip into a doorway of the science building. Travis spotted him at the same instant hurrying towards them, and greeted him with his usual knowing leer as Gilpin came up, panting a bit from his exertion. "My, my, *such* heavy breathing, and so early in the day."

"Cut it out, Eric. You could at least have held on a minute and introduced me."

"I am not my physicist's keeper. Whither the luscious Anika goeth, I shall not follow. Selah."

"Say, Eric," Gilpin began, failing miserably in his effort to sound casual, "you haven't seen Julie around the last few days, have you?"

"Julie? Oh dear, you *must* be needing your horns trimmed a bit on the urgent side if you are looking in *that* direction."

"Eric. Can you just answer my question?"

"Julie and I have not been seeing eye to eye. She has said some most unprofessional things about me."

"Yes, but do you know if she's gone somewhere or something? Or had some family emergency?"

"Family emergency? I should have thought she was originally produced in some very risky genetic engineering experiment. I mean, do frozen embryos have families?"

"I don't know why I bother trying to have a serious conversation with you." Travis beamed with undiminished amusement. A thought occurred to Gilpin. "What exactly was your fight with her about, anyway?" he asked.

"Well, since you are *so* insistent on my being serious, I *will* illuminate you about that. You know she was trying this *ridiculous* business to start an interdisciplinary course on what she was quaintly calling 'world *literature*' while I was acting chairman last year, just after the department was founded and before our dear chair arrived. Well I mean, really, the whole thing was *everything* that we've been struggling against. So logocentric to be privileging *texts*. I for one was utterly relieved to be out of that moldy literature department, which was just *crawling* with people who *love* literature. It was so retro.

"And here she was directly undermining me and my authority

by going out and getting five thousand dollars added to the budget for this ridiculous course."

"So what happened? I know the course was cancelled."

"Well of course it was cancelled, since I had to put my foot down and reprogram that money to a more appropriate purpose."

"And what was that?"

"I had every right to do so."

A light went on in Gilpin's head. "You put it in your queer studies program, didn't you?"

"It was my decision to make. And she made such a fuss just because I didn't tell her about it right away."

"Okay, Eric. But you don't know anything about where she is? Apparently she hasn't been to class for a couple of days and hasn't been at home, either."

"Probably having an attack of the vapors. You know, for all her screwing-in-Shakespeare studies, she's *very* Victorian. And a bit whacko."

✤ 3.

Gilpin made his way back up the creaking stairs of Trojan Hall to the third floor and turned left down the corridor where the D-CADS department offices had all now been consolidated. His footsteps set the recycling bins at the end of the corridor rattling, but otherwise all was a sepulchral quiet.

Everyone else was still at The Blue Olive, Gilpin guessed, fortifying themselves for their afternoon classes. There was no glow of fluorescent light coming from any of the frosted transoms of his colleagues' offices as he passed the dark oak doors, each labeled with a small white-lettered nameplate: Doe, Shalaby, Glantz, Travis, Heatherton, Bariki.

Well, Shalaby was no doubt in—he was there all hours, an odor of illicit cigarette smoke perpetually wafting from his office, a DO NOT DISTURB sign lifted from some hotel hanging on the doorknob: the department's mystery man and recluse, whose stock in trade was anger at the crimes of the Zionists.

The few times Gilpin had spoken to him, it had been hard to tell whether Shalaby was angrier at the crimes of the Zionists or with the fact that the rest of the world was not as angry as he was at the crimes of the Zionists.

He kept a strange collection of odds and ends of spent American ordnance and other military hardware in his office—tank shells, the fins of a smashed air-to-ground missile, a night vision scope, and a particularly nasty looking commando knife—that he said were proof of Western complicity in the crimes of the Zionists. Gilpin would have to tackle him eventually for his inquiry, but didn't feel he could face it now.

He had his key in the door of his office and was turning the knob when a furious scratching sound, followed by a muffled obscenity, emanated from the office across the corridor. Gilpin went over and knocked on the door, which was hung with a red, gold, and green weaving that spelled out BARIKI in much larger letters than the university-supplied nameplate. A voice answered, but the words were obscured by an explosion of barks. Gilpin opened the door cautiously. A small black Scottie shot across the room, barking with all the fury of a small dog on a mission. Gilpin did a sort of crazed dance trying to evade the dog's lunging forays at his ankles.

A man in a long gold dashiki and an elaborate string of carvings around his neck made his way rapidly out from behind the desk, alternately shouting, "Get down Tyrone. Get down you little motherfucker" to the dog and "What the hell's matter with you man, why you upsetting my dog" to Gilpin. He finally grabbed the dog's collar and hauled him out of sight behind his desk. A subdued obligatto of growls emerged from the vicinity of the file drawer.

"Jesus, Mfuka, why do you have to keep bringing your dog into the office."

"What, now you against me too, man? You on the bitch's side? That bitch is gonna be sorry she messed with me."

"No, I'm *not* against you Mfuka. I'm staying out of this one. But look you have to admit Tyrone's a bit on the aggressive side. I mean think of the liability issues if he bites a student or someone."

"Hell, he don't bite nobody." The growling continued. "You know what that bitch is saying now?" he asked, his tone one of sheer incredulity. "She's saying she's got some fucking multiple chemical sensitivity disorder and she got a note from her doctor that if some dog got flea spray on his ass six months ago, it's still a *theeee*-ret to her damn health."

"I know—she was talking to Welch about it at the meeting this morning. Where were you, by the way?"

"Shit, man, I don't got time to go to no meetings with the Frosted Flake. Anyway, she got some note from *her* doctor, I got a note from my fucking canine behavioral therapist that Tyrone's got eating disorders and separation anxiety so he's got to have his *ass* in *here* with *me*."

"Look, Mfuka, I wanted to ask you. Have you seen Julie lately? Nobody seems to have seen her for a few days and well, Welch asked me if I would just sort of informally ask around and see if anyone knew where she had gone."

"No man, I ain't seen her this week at all. Shit, she probably had it up to her ass with *Doctor* fucking John Doe's cognitive fucking semiotics and decided to get her fucking ass out of here." He paused for a second and gave the dog's collar a sharp tug. "Flake talk about his plan for sponsoring courses and all that at that meeting?"

"Oh, you heard about that. It was news to me. And, look, Mfuka we really need to get organized and protest this. In fact that's the other thing I wanted to talk to you about."

Bariki snorted. "You know what this whole bullshit of putting us into this new department with *Doctor* fucking John Doe as the man is about, don't you?"

"Well, uh, no Mfuka, not really. I mean I don't really think much of cognitive semiotics but it is sort of the hot trend in the field. Isn't it?"

"Oh man are you *niiii*-eave. Look we got fucking tenure, right?"

"Well of course."

"So the Frosted Flake can't fire our asses, right?"

"Right."

"But he can make our lives so fucking miserable we'll be begging to go. Coz we're what stands between *him* and his plan of 'making the college more businesslike.' Right? I mean he knows no fucking C-E-O with a pole up his white ass is going to want to put his fucking company's name on the courses *we* teach, right? So that's why he puts this dumb ass in charge with all this shit about making the humanities into some pro-to Human Science. I tell you, man, if that *Doctor* fucking John Doe comes in here *one* more time with his fucking theories about cognitive fucking semiotics and 'meaning negotiation' in African-American music, I am going to *bust* his fucking ass. But I am keeping *my* ass right here." He gave another furious yank on the dog's collar, and the growling finally stopped. "And Tyrone's too."

Gilpin said nothing for a moment. "Mfuka, can I ask you something?"

"Sure, man."

"It's uh, well kind of personal."

"What, you think I'm some kind of pansy and I'm gonna go ooh-ooh-ooh you ask me some personal question? Go ahead and ask, man."

"You're sure you won't mind?"

"Ask the fucking question, man."

"Okay." He took a deep breath. "When you were appointed here, the gazette ran your bio. It said you grew up in Hanover, New Hampshire, right?"

"So what?"

Tyrone began to growl again.

"So—it said your father's one of the leading cardiac surgeons in the whole country. Your mother has a Ph.D. in library science. You went to Harvard and to graduate school at Princeton."

"Yeah?"

" So *why* do you put on this act?"

"Man, you ask some fucking personal questions. What you talking about?"

Gilpin put his head in his hand. "Oh geez, I knew this would happen. But I mean, well for chrissake the made-up African name and the dashiki—I mean, Jesus Christ, Mfuka—Huey Newton doesn't even wear a dashiki anymore. Marion Barry doesn't wear a dashiki anymore."

"Huey Newton don't wear no fucking dashiki *any* more because Huey Newton is fucking *dead*, man."

"Okay, but you know what I mean. You talk like a parody, not like someone who wrote his Ph.D. thesis on Kant, for chrissake."

Bariki got up, picking up the Scottie in his arms, walked to the door and cautiously looked up and down the corridor. Gilpin had never seen anyone outside of a bad spy movie do that. He returned to his desk and sat down. "Okay man, I'll tell you. But you just keep it to yourself, okay? You got *any* idea how hard it is to get black students to take African-American studies these days? All they want is pre-law, and marketing, and chemical engineering. Little money-grubbing assholes. Shit, there was just some article in the *Chronicle* with a bunch of black students going '*so-ci-e-ty* won't take me *se-ri-ous-ly* if I take black studies.'

"So you know what you do? You beg them and you go through all this shit about their heritage and all the famous fucking black astronauts and doctors and money-grubbing asshole CEOs who majored in African-American studies and it didn't hurt them any and then they finally sign up for your class and then they fill out the fucking student evaluation at the end and all they can say is you act 'too white.' So shit, man, the Frosted Flake want me to *dee*-light the customers, I am going to *dee*-light the customers."

He paused. "I tell you what, I find that honky motherfucker who came up with student evaluations, I am going to kick his ass from here to the North Pole."

"Okay, well, look, Mfuka, if you hear anything about Julie, will you let me know?"

"Sure thing, man."

Gilpin's phone was ringing as he again unlocked his office door. It was the smallest office on the floor, but it made up for that with its corner location and windows that gave unobstructed views to the southeast and southwest, admitting sunlight even in winter, and dispelling some of the Gothic gloom that pervaded most of the building. A few healthier-than-usual-looking large cacti stood on the windowsill, and a small, bright red oriental carpet covered the floor in front of the desk. Blond-finished maple bookshelves, a cut above the university issue, lined the walls, the shelves filled with orange-backed Penguin paperback editions of all the "classics" he had devoured as a student; not that anyone called them that anymore. An incongruously old-fashioned wing chair covered in a faded paisley fabric kept the room from looking too modernistically fussy.

Gilpin picked up the phone on the sixth ring.

"Hello—Theodore?" a voice asked doubtfully.

"Yes, mom, who *else* would it be?"

"Oh, thank goodness. I know I'm just an old lady but you know I read an article in *USA Today* about a man who was tied up in his office for four days by a bunch of shtarkers who answered the phone and pretended to be him while they went and took all his money out from his ATM machine. So I'm just saying, you should be careful."

"Mom, nobody is going to get tied up in their office here. I'm fine."

"Well, someday you'll have children, and you'll worry too, and maybe you won't think your mother is being so silly."

"Okay, look, mom, I've got to go. I'll call you later."

"And speaking of children, I know it's none of my business, but I'm just saying maybe if you tried a little to become chairman of your department and made some more money and got a nicer car, you might meet some nice girl."

"Mom, my car is fine. And anyway I keep telling you, nobody tries to be chairman of a university department. All it is is headaches and it takes time away from your own work—writing articles and so forth."

"Well, I'm sure you know best. I'm just your mother. But, Theodore, you know I couldn't even show my friends that last article you sent me. I know I should be proud, but that whole magazine, all the articles had such dirty titles. Feh."

"Look, mom, I promise, I'll call you later," he said, and quickly hung up.

He rubbed his forehead. Welch had asked him to look around Julie's office but now that he thought about it he wasn't sure what the legality of that was. He supposed it was all right—university property and all. Could Doe lend him the key if he explained what it was about?

He took out a pad of paper and wrote "Last seen by," "When," and "Where" at the top of three columns, then underlined each one. Immediately feeling ridiculous, he tore the sheet off, crumpled it up, threw it in a line drive into the basket against the wall, tossed the pad down on his desk, and headed for the door.

He was driven back at once into the center of the room, however, by Wendy Heatherton, who had come barreling through the door at that instant saying, "I need to talk to *you*." She closed the door behind her and stood with her arms crossed in front of it.

"Wendy, I'd love to talk to you but I have something I need to do right now," Gilpin said apologetically.

"I'm going to talk to you, and I'm not going to be silenced by power ploys. I thought I would have been able to count on you to speak out against patriarchal attempts to 'keep women in their place' by labeling them 'hysterical.' I would have thought after the years of struggle to establish fragrance and chemical-free zones in meeting rooms at this university that we were past the point where we would still be fighting to raise consciousnesses about multiple chemical sensitivity disorder. But I see I was mistaken."

Wendy Heatherton, McAllister Lawless Professor of Rhetoric and Power, was the oldest member of the D-CADS department, in her mid-40s, but nearly always dressed like an undergraduate on a warm spring day.

She wore painfully tight faded jeans that sank down to her hips and a tank top with a complicated combination of shoulder straps that bared a substantial area of back and cleavage, and even a small band of midriff. Her coarse dark hair was put up in one of the sloppy pony tails that were the universal style among the women students that year.

She was not unattractive; but there was something slightly grotesque about the overall effect. Towards men she habitually projected an air of superior scorn at the sexual power she held over them. Gilpin had long ago realized there was no way he could even subtly disabuse her of the idea.

"Wendy, I'm sorry. I can just see both sides of this issue and I decided I can't get involved in this."

"So you're just going to acquiesce in the perpetuation of gender stereotyping."

"Look, I've got Mfuka yelling at me and I've got you yelling at me and you know I've always opposed gender bias at the university. And exposed it in my research and teaching as well." Gilpin felt as sanctimonious and unconvincing as he always did when forced to bear witness to his credentials as a sensitive and unprejudiced, if nonetheless unavoidably male, member of the academic community.

"Between the illegal smoking and the *multiple* pet allergens it's now impossible for me to spend more than a few minutes a day in my office. That is a totally unacceptable situation." Gilpin decided not to mention the fact that she had never spent more than a few minutes a day at her office.

Heatherton's expression took on a smirk. "But maybe since you're now doing little special jobs as Welch's bum boy, you've decided not to make waves."

"How on earth—"

"Oh, don't think I don't know what goes on at this place. But what I want *you* to tell me, since you're playing boy detective, is what this little project is Julie Glantz has been working on so obsessively for the last few months."

"I honestly have no idea. And I'm not playing any kind of detective. Welch just asked me to ask everyone if they knew where she might be. But do you think her project could have something to with her, uh, not being around for the last few days?"

"She's obviously lost it. Not that *she* was ever what she claimed to be. She went around calling herself a 'post-feminist feminist' and even had the *balls* to put on her website that *she* was the 'Camille Paglia with balls' of the D-CADS department, when everyone knows that's what people have been calling *me* for years. She's not even a pre-feminist feminist."

"But wait a minute, Wendy, I sat in on the seminar she gave last spring to the music department and I mean it was all very avant garde stuff. It was all about Bach's patriarchal objectification of key structures. She even called the *Well-Tempered Clavier* a 'rape manual.'"

"Just posturing," Heatherton sneered. "And all this crap about her working class upbringing as a victim of patriarchal abuse. She's got family money somewhere, and I bet a rich daddy that she twisted around her finger and who dotes on her."

"Oh, come on, she drives that ancient VW bug. And she brings sandwiches for lunch. And she has that awful little apartment. I mean she certainly doesn't act like someone with inherited wealth."

"*She's* a poseur of the first order. You'll see." She put her hands on the front edge of Gilpin's desk and leaned toward him, giving him a far fuller view of her ample breasts than he wanted. "Don't think I'm through with you, either," she whispered, in a tone he guessed was meant to be both provocative and menacing; then turned in a sort of sweeping, nineteenth-century grande-dame exit that would have been more impressive if it hadn't been so at odds with her skimpy wardrobe.

Gilpin let out a huge sigh, got up from his desk, and realized he was walking to his door like a sapper treading gingerly through a minefield, bracing himself for the next explosion. He resumed a more normal stride, locked the door behind him, and headed down the corridor.

He paused at Glantz's door and looked at it feeling he ought to be able to discern some tiny but momentous clue. A scrap of sticky tape on the door caught his eye and as he reached up to touch it the door swung open a crack. He cautiously pushed a bit harder and it swung all the way open.

He closed the door quietly behind him, locked it, and, acutely conscious of feeling like a parody of a mystery-novel detective, let his eyes wander over the room. The floor was piled with stacks of folders, student papers, and books—all much as he remembered from the last time he had been in here.

His eye fell on a card on heavy stock, emblazoned with a deep red fox's head, protruding prominently from a book halfway down one pile. Gilpin carefully slid it out. "Xenia Hounds Annual Hunt Ball, December 13," it read. "Black tie. Scarlet if convenient."

He turned it over. A series of words in nearly illegible handwriting covered the back. He puzzled over the script for several minutes before finally deciphering "granola," "plain yogurt," "t.p." He hastily slid the card back where he had found it and decided not to disturb the piles.

Hesitating, he switched on her computer.

When the screen came up it was covered with little yellow squares designed to look like sticky notes. In all of them the words "Publish or perish" were written. Gilpin sat down at the desk and, feeling like a criminal, began to look through the items on the computer desktop. A calendar was entirely blank except for an entry on the previous Thursday which read, "tour chapel organ 3 pm—call Joe Dwight."

Her email outbox had no messages more recent than last Friday.

The inbox was jammed with offers for low-interest mortgages and products to extend the length of one's "manhood," and one lengthy, weepy note from a student pleading for a higher grade on a paper which concluded, "It's especially stressful to me because this class counts for BOTH my majors!!!"

But one message caused the nerves at the back of his neck to creep. It was dated just yesterday, and had not yet been opened. The real sender's name was obviously obscured by someone who knew how to do that—it was made to appear that Glantz was both sender and receiver. "YOUR TURN'S COMING" the message read in all capitals.

And beneath that:

HOW LONG CAN YOU KEEP UP THIS FRAUD, BITCH? AND BY THE WAY, IN WHICH WAY WOULD YOU SAY YOU ARE MORE FRUSTRATED: INTELLECTUALLY OR SEXUALLY?

And then, lastly, what appeared to be a quotation in Latin:

tristius haud illis monstrum, nec saeuior ulla
pestis et ira deum Stygiis sese extulit undis.
Virginei volucrum vultus, foedissima ventris
proluvies uncaeque manus et pallida semper
ora fame.

Who knew Latin anymore? He didn't think Glantz possibly could. He certainly didn't. There was something vaguely familiar about the quotation nonetheless. He glanced over at the printer, hit control-P, wincing at the sound as the page printed out.

At the same moment footsteps came down the corridor. They paused briefly just outside Glantz's door. Gilpin froze. Then the steps reversed direction, back toward the stairway.

Damn, Gilpin thought.

His hands felt clammy. He rapidly scrolled through the rest of the messages from the last week. Nothing else stood out except for a message sent the previous Thursday from someone whose email address was nothing but a string of meaningless letters and numbers, and which was written, somewhat unusually, in the form of an extremely old-fashioned, formal letter:

> My dear Professor Glantz:
>
> I am most concerned at the lack of progress reports from you on our project.
> If you have decided to abandon **GREAT JEWISH FOXHUNTERS**, please have the minimal courtesy to let me know. In either case, I expect you to turn over your drafts and notes, given the considerable sum I have invested in this enterprise to date.
>
> Yours most sincerely,
> Your True Friend and Admirer

He read it again to see if there was some joke he was missing. "Great Jewish Foxhunters" certainly had the ring of an ironic, postmodern jouissance.

He tried searching on the hard drive for the words "great jewish foxhunters," but came up blank. He switched off the computer, looked at all the piles of papers and books, and decided maybe he would take just a quick glance through. It was harder work than he thought, especially since he had to admit he didn't even know what he was looking for. An hour and a hour later he hadn't found anything having any connection to Jews, foxhunters, G., or much of anything else but the usual dross and detritus of teaching and administration.

Feeling more like a crook than ever, he skulked out the door, closing it with excruciating care behind him to avoid making a sound.

✤ 4.

A vague smell of stale cigarette smoke greeted Gilpin when he arrived home. A note, written on what he realized with horror was the title page torn from one of his books, sat on the kitchen counter.

> Professer I couldn't do the bath rooms or bed rooms this week also your cofee thing is broke Tonya

The late afternoon sun slanting through the living room windows illuminated in sharp relief a six-inch-wide band of dust that framed the edge of the room and various pieces of furniture with a chiaroscuro effect. The piano occupied an island of dust all to itself, like a lone palm emerging from a tropical key.

Gilpin switched on the music player he had downloaded with a random assortment of pieces that he liked to listen to when he was too tired and irritated even to have to decide for himself what to hear, and sank down into one of the armchairs. The sounds of a Bach chorale prelude filled the room; a quiet, wistful, almost Romantic ostinato in the left hand and pedals drawn from the chorale melody itself, then the plaintive hymn tune entering in the right hand, weaving in and out of its echoing accompaniment. It was in a major key but full of half-resolved suspensions and occasional odd chromatic darts into the minor that just as quickly returned to major, somehow creating more of a feeling of unfulfilled longing than if it had been in a minor key altogether.

A title came into his mind, *An Wasserflüssen Babylon*—Psalm 137. *By the rivers of Babylon, there we sat down, and yea we wept, when we remembered Zion.* So strange to think of a German Lutheran setting such a haunting arrangement of the words of the Hebrew Bible, the Babylonian captives lamenting the loss of Jerusalem.

The chorale melody had just made its last entrance and was heading for the final, quiet resolution when the off-key electronic ringing of the telephone jarringly intruded.

"Damn," Gilpin said out loud. He got up, switched off the music, and picked up the phone, practically barking "hello" with undisguised irritation.

"Oh, thank goodness. Theodore. It's your mother."

"Yes, mom, I recognize your voice."

"You said you were going to call me back, but when I tried calling your office there was no answer. So I worried."

"I was going to call you back. I had some things to do and I left early. In fact, mom, can I call you a little later—I still have some things I need to do."

"Maybe you're going somewhere tonight?"

"No mom, I've just got to prepare for my class tomorrow. Look I'll call you this evening, really. I promise. Okay? Bye."

He restarted the player at the beginning of the piece but the mood was broken. He picked up the poetry anthology that he made the students in his Burns and Burns class buy in the hopes they might broaden their appreciation of poetry just a bit, and flipped to the poem they were doing tomorrow.

> *It was upon a Lammas night,*
> *When corn rigs are bonie,*
> *Beneath the moon's unclouded light,*
> *I held awa to Annie;*
> *The time flew by, wi' tentless heed,*
> *Till, 'tween the late and early*

Wi' sma' persuasion she agreed
To see me thro' the barley.

God, he wondered what Wendy Heatherton would say about that. But didn't the naïve beauty of the poem's vignette count for something? Wasn't there a place for dreams of innocence and love and young passion and the magic of being lost to the world under the stars even amid structuralism and feminist criticism? Christ, if he started talking to his students about love and innocence and stars what would *they* even think—all so cynical and matter-of-fact about sex and "relationships," as they invariably called it. He couldn't remember hearing any of them ever using the word love in any serious context. He'd once made the mistake of telling one of his students she needed to "hook up" with another for an assignment they were working on and was met with a bunch of snickers, and then a student after class very seriously and patiently "explaining" to him what the term meant; as if he didn't know what sex was, either.

He idly flipped through the anthology; so many love poems, mostly written by men true enough, most either feeling sorry for themselves or urging the lassies to give way to them.

Gather ye rosebuds while ye may,
Old Time is still a-flying

Inevitably, he thought of the parody of the next two lines:

And what you get for free today,
Tomorrow you'll be buying.

Maybe it *was* all masculine hypocrisy, all that talk of love just an elaborate con to get girls to put out. Maybe this generation was more honest. He turned over a few more pages.

Had we but world enough, and time,
This coyness, Lady, were no crime...
But at my back I always hear
Time's wingèd chariot hurrying near...
The grave's a fine and private place,
But none, I think, do there embrace.

Dammit. He threw the book down and picked up the cryptic crossword puzzle he had been struggling with all week. 19 across. Poet composed sonnet about New York (8).

He stared at it for a few minutes The only result was the beginnings of a dull ache in his forehead. He got up and looked up de Groot in the campus directory and picked up the phone. There was no dial tone.

After a second's pause a voice came from the receiver.

"Hello—Theodore?"

"Mom, for God's sake."

"Your phone didn't even ring. Maybe there's something wrong with it?"

"No, mom. I was just picking up the phone to call someone."

"I don't mean to pry, but maybe you're calling some nice girl and asking her out already?"

"Okay, mom, yes, that's exactly what I'm doing. So if you can just not keep calling me, I can call her. That ought to make you happy, right?"

"You don't have to talk to your mother that way. Now, you know, Theodore, I know you think people my age don't know about these things, but I read in *People* magazine that some Hollywood person got this terrible infection doing a certain thing that the young people are doing these days. So I just wanted to say, that if you get serious with this girl, you need to be careful because even nice girls can have this problem without even knowing it. Okay? So maybe you should take an antibiotic just to be on the safe side."

"Oh, God, mom, for chrissake. I'm just going to ask her to have a cup of coffee with me. Believe it or not, men and women do just go out for a cup of coffee these days. Now look this is so embarrassing when you say things like this."

"Well, I'm just saying you should remember your uncle Alvin. Everyone thought he was fine, and then he went to the doctor and they found he had gall bladder, and two weeks later he was gone, just like that. And such a young man."

"Mom, Alvin was eighty-three. And—what on earth does he have to do with this?"

"Alright, if you don't care about your relatives, that's alright. I never push."

"Goodbye, mom."

He pushed the receiver hook down and waited a few seconds then abruptly lifted it, greatly relieved to hear the dial tone. He punched the number. He felt a lurch in his stomach when he heard her answer, "Anika de Groot."

"Oh, hello. This is Ted Gilpin." His voice had uncontrollably risen at the end of the sentence, turning it into something that sounded like a question.

There was an embarrassing pause. "I'm sorry, do I know you?"

Oh, God, Gilpin thought. "Um, Ted Gilpin. I'm in the D-CADS department. I'm the guy who made an ass of himself at the meeting this morning?"

She laughed, in all a rather pleasant laugh, he thought. "Oh, I'm sorry," she said.

"Sorry you didn't recognize me, or sorry I made an ass of myself?"

She laughed again. "Sorry I didn't recognize you. I know who you are now."

"Well, good. Great. Look, I was wondering if you'd like to, uh, get a cup of coffee."

"When?" She said it in a perfectly neutral and noncommittal

way that implied she was doing nothing more than collecting data.

He almost lost his nerve completely and said "oh, any time" when the words *Time's wingèd chariot* came floating back through his thoughts. "Right now?"

"I'm rather busy right now." Well, that's it, Gilpin thought. "But if you can wait until nine," she continued, "I should be finished. Though I've rather noticed that no one in the humanities seems to keep those kinds of hours, so maybe you'll be long gone by then."

"Well, to be honest with you, I'm at home now. But I only live a few blocks from campus. So nine is great. Perfect," he quickly added, suddenly afraid she might say something about not wanting him to trouble himself. "So I'll meet you at Java Java Java Java at nine then?"

"I will look forward to it," she said, with a touch of Old World formality that strangely touched him.

Whew, Gilpin thought as he replaced the receiver. Idiotic I should still feel like I'm in junior high school when I just call a colleague for a perfectly ordinary, natural, thing like grabbing a cup of coffee. Yeah, right, he thought. Nothing natural about it in the least. For one thing she was brilliant, beautiful, and must have certainly concluded that he was a total ass.

The phone rang. He snatched it up furiously. "Mom, I do *not* want to hear one more word about Uncle Alvin's gall bladder. I do not want to hear one more word about people being tied to their desks. And I *definitely* do not want to hear one more word about the practices of Hollywood celebrities and the various resulting loathsome diseases they have contracted. Is that perfectly clear?"

There was a pause, and a deep baritone voice spoke. "Is this Professor Theodore Gilpin speaking?"

"Oh geez. I'm sorry. I thought you were someone else."

"So I had divined, Professor Gilpin. Please think nothing of it. This *is* Professor Gilpin?"

"Yes it is. Who's calling?"

"Perhaps we might just refer to myself as 'G.' for the moment."

"Oh—G. As in—G."

"That is *quite* correct, Professor Gilpin. I see you comprehend completely. I believe *you* may have something that *I* am interested in. Something in the form of a manuscript? A possibly incomplete, yet still most valuable—valuable to me, though perhaps to no one else—manuscript? Something that is without a doubt rightfully mine. But which has to my considerable displeasure eluded me."

"I'm afraid I don't know what you're talking about."

"Oh, don't you, Professor Gilpin? Well, perhaps. Or, perhaps not. I should very much like to meet you in any case. It would be an honor. Distinguished professor. Scholar of the humanities. Expert on the *detective* novel. Shall we say my hotel tonight? I am staying at the *Ramada* Inn. Not exactly the level of comfort one would expect, but convenient for my purposes. Tell me what time would suit you."

"Um, look, this is all a bit odd."

"Yes, I suppose it is." He chuckled. "Well, let me say, while I think you may have something I want, but I am also confident that *I* have something *you* want. And that something is, shall I say, information? About a certain colleague of yours who has not been seen? So please tell me when I shall expect you."

Gilpin's mind was reeling. This was straight out of *The Maltese Falcon*. Was it a practical joke? "Alright, Eric, I know it's you. Cut it out."

"Professor Gilpin," the voice continued—it would have been hard for Travis to drop his voice an octave and a half, Gilpin realized as soon as he had said it—"I can perfectly well understand your perplexity and surprise, but I can assure you I am who I say I am. This is not one of your colleagues playing a jest upon you."

"Okay, I'll be there at eleven. How will I recognize you?"

"I will be in the lounge. I am a somewhat corpulent man. You will not miss me. Until then."

Gilpin filled the time until nine o'clock cooking himself a mushroom omelet, attempting to reattach the handle on his espresso machine that his cleaning lady had broken off, and rereading Burns and trying not to think of Anika. He found himself glancing at the clock every two minutes. Finally, at twenty til, he gave up, pulled on his jacket, and strode the three blocks to campus, getting there fifteen minutes early. He walked around the block twice, then plunged into Java Java Java Java.

The coffee shop was crowded with the usual crush of students and the ageing counter-culture types that congregated around university towns working in the bookstores, bicycle shops, and used-clothing stores.

Most of the students were sitting by themselves at tables, scowling glumly at laptops, their styrofoam cups holding an inch or two of the tepid remains of hours-old caramel and whipped cream concoctions that somehow were considered coffee these days. Of course Anika wasn't there yet. Gilpin ordered a small decaf skim latte, which the server, as always, informed him was actually a tall decaf no-fat latte, and found an empty table in the far corner.

He tried not to keep looking at his watch or gulping down his coffee but failed at both, and his cup was practically empty when she walked through the door twenty-five minutes later, at exactly 9:15.

She waved to him, motioned that she was going to get herself something, and after what seemed like an interminable wait while the heavily tattooed barrista finished with a half-dozen particularly elaborate drinks in huge cups involving syrups, whipped cream, extra shots, and chocolate sprinkles, and made her way over to his table.

Feeling strangely old-fashioned yet somehow perfectly right, he found himself formally standing up, shaking her hand, and pulling a chair out for her as she joined him. "I'm sorry I'm late," she said, raising her eyebrows and shrugging her shoulders slightly as if to suggest it was merely some unaccountable quirk of fate.

"Oh it's fine. I just got here myself," he lied.

She laughed her small melodious laugh and said, sarcastically but not at all unkindly, "Oh, so that's why your cup is empty. Or are you the world's fastest coffee drinker?"

"Okay, so I lied. I've been waiting forty-five minutes. But it's fine. Really. It's nice to see you—well, to meet you, really."

"So, you are another one of these great modern literary theorists like Eric Travis?" she asked, the tone of amusement still in her voice.

"I think Eric is sui generis," he replied, wondering if she also was asking whether he was gay.

"So you don't explain everything by its inner structure and insist there is no such thing as outer reality?"

"No, I don't go quite as far as Eric. He does get a little carried away."

"Yes, he was explaining to me this afternoon Lacan's theory that the square root of minus 1 signifies the male erectile organ. I had to tell him that I had never noticed the resemblance myself."

"No, uh, me neither, I suppose." He laughed nervously. "I suppose where I agree with Eric—and well, with everyone really who does literature these days—is that you do need a basis in theory to advance the field. I mean we can't just sit around reading Shakespeare over and over again. And really all that structuralism says is that meaning is conditioned on structure, and that privileging any one viewpoint based on the claim that it commands an absolute external reality is suspect. I mean, after all, that's no different from what modern physics tells us, isn't it? Chaos theory, indeterminacy, Heisenberg's Uncertainty Principle—I mean, if the observer affects what appears to be 'reality' by the very act of observing, how can you still claim that there is any such thing as absolute reality or absolute truth?"

Anika grimaced.

"You know, I have been thinking of starting an organization dedicated to the extermination of idiotic statements about Heisenberg from humanists. Why is it that none of you can ever get this right?"

Gilpin looked nonplussed. "Why—what did I say that was wrong? That *is* the Uncertainty Principle isn't it—that the observer alters the experiment?"

Anika shook her head with a slow sarcastic smile. "Perhaps you would like to enroll in Physics for Poets? The Uncertainty Principle says that the uncertainty in the location of a particle times the uncertainty in its momentum is always greater than a certain small constant. So if you know the location very precisely, you cannot know the momentum so accurately. And the other way around: if you know the momentum accurately, you cannot know the location so accurately. But first of all this is significant only in the case of very small particles—things on a quantum scale. It has nothing whatever to do with day to day life, as for example even literature professors experience it. And second, it is complete bullshit the way people try to claim the Uncertainty Principle says that the observer always alters reality."

"Oh."

"But maybe you are not a poet, either? Isn't the whole purpose of the humanities these days to prove that poetry—and art and music and anything else a person might have the effrontery to actually enjoy—are a patriarchal construct?"

"Ouch. That's a bit unfair. I mean, I went into this field because I loved books and poetry—and music. But we have to be relevant. We surely have to progress with the times, just as science does. And in fact we're moving in a very exciting direction of fusing the humanities and science."

"Relevant? All you are doing is destroying the only thing the arts had in their favor. You have read C. P. Snow—*The Masters*? Then, when was it, the 1950s, the great culture war in the university was between the cool progress of science and the warm tradition of the humanities.

"But now you in the humanities try to cloak yourself with a jargon and a kind of pseudo-methodology of science—stripping it of any actual scientific meaning in the process, just like you just did with poor Heisenberg—and then you spend your time spinning 'theories' whose only effect is to drain the beauty out of literature, and art, and music, and poetry which is the only reason it ever mattered in the first place. It is not as if art is ever going to cure a disease or explore the planets or clean up polluted streams or grow more food for the world, I mean.

"Yet you are all only really happy when you are exposing great art as some sexist, classist, racist, or imperialist plot. So you don't have the science, you don't have progress, but you also don't even have the warmth or the tradition any more."

"Well, it's rather a quaint and questionable idea that 'beauty' is a valid or defensible concept," Gilpin said, starting to get a bit vexed under Anika's relentless attack, "or that it should even be the purpose of art. And the very act of transgressing traditional boundaries has often exposed some of the societal forces that created all of these problems you mentioned in the first place. I mean look at the power of the muckrakers—*The Jungle.* And the Dadaists. And—"

He found himself groping for another example. "And protest music."

"Oh, yes. A friend gave me that old record by the satirist—Tom Lehrer? He had a very funny line about protest music. 'They may have won all the battles, but we had all the good songs.'"

"But, look, you're not dismissing the importance of scholarship itself in advancing the cause of women and minorities and exposing entrenched biases? You were arguing yourself today to Welch that more needs to be done for women in the sciences."

"Do you think I want more opportunity for women in the sciences because I want us to do some girlie physics?"

"Okay. Tell me why you went into physics."

"Okay," she said, mocking his tone back to him. "I loved math. I loved its beauty and order. It was the closest thing to God

I had ever seen in the real world. I remember one professor I had, he made a joke, he was showing us the Taylor series and—"

"Uh, what's that?"

"Taylor series? It's an expansion, an infinite series that defines the value of any function at a small distance away from a known value. And the amazing thing, as this professor was pointing out to us and trying to make us see, is the way it is so astonishingly symmetrical.

"I mean, there is no reason on earth you would expect such a powerful and universal formula to be so ordered or to even take the form it does.

"But you go through all this long derivation, and out falls this, well, work of art. The first term is just the function F at x. The next term is delta x times the first derivative of F at x divided by one factorial. The next term is delta x squared times the second derivative of F at x divided by 2 factorial. And so on. The first term zeroth power, zeroth derivative, zero factorial; the next term 1, 1, 1; the next 2, 2, 2; the next 3, 3, 3, and so on forever. Now why should that be?"

"And so what was the joke your professor made?"

"He wrote it all out on the board and he was trying to get us to see how beautiful and astonishing this was. And he finally said, 'I mean look at this—entire religions have been based less than this.' Of course seven-eighths of the class were guys from China, so I was the only one who laughed." She smiled. "He was kidding, but I am not sure I am.

"And then," she continued, "when mathematics and physics come together there is nothing that makes you feel so much that you are touching the truth of the universe. Yet it happens all the time. You set up an equation describing the physical forces, and it's messy and obscure and then you find a way to simplify it and all of a sudden you have a clear formula that expresses a basic law of cause and effect, things you never knew before.

"And why should an equation, why should the machinery of

mathematics, know what you, who wrote the equation yourself, did not? But you test out the formula, and it works. It predicts what will happen, every time." She was speaking with more passion than he had heard in her voice before. "You can't do that in the arts. And why should you want to?"

"I don't know." He had been gazing at his empty cup while she was speaking but now he looked up and gave her a sheepish grin. "I have to ask you," he began, "—you have"—he started to say "a beautiful voice" but caught himself—"you sound like you must be a singer. Are you?"

"Yes, I sang in college, and before that, when I was a girl, in the church choir."

"Where was that?"

"Oh, just a little town outside Amsterdam, but there is a beautiful baroque church with an organ built by Schnitger. You know, who built some of the organs Bach himself played in Germany. And we sang Bach, and Palestrina, and I don't think I ever believed in God for a minute, but I felt for that music the same thing I felt for mathematics."

Gilpin glanced at his watch with a start. "Oh, geez, I'm really sorry—I have to go. I'm—well I've got to take care of something I promised to do. Look, I just wanted to say that I, well, I really admired the way you stood up to Welch at that meeting, and I feel like a complete idiot for the way I handled myself."

She smiled, no sarcasm this time, nothing but sympathetic understanding. "You shouldn't feel sorry. You cared about the truth, and that's what matters. You know, for all you say about not believing there is such a thing as absolute truth, or beauty, I think you know that is total bullshit."

"Okay," he said, "I'll see you," and walked to the door with a feeling of exaltation that would have convinced even a reprobate like Eric Travis that there was such a thing as truth and beauty, or the most cynical sophomore in his poetry class that there was such a thing as love.

✤ 5.

The elderly combo in burgundy dinner jackets had just finished hacking their way through a very loud and upbeat rendition of "Strangers in the Night" and the sound of six hands clapping arose from the Wednesday night assembly of software salesmen drinking at solitary tables as Gilpin walked into the Ramada's Boilermaker Room.

A man in a well-made suit, hugely overweight even by Midwestern American standards, sat at a table near the door, as far away from the band as possible. He had a large red face and heavy jowls that made Gilpin think of an elderly bloodhound. Gilpin approached him a bit uncertainly, but the man immediately rose and grasped his hand. "Ah, Professor Gilpin, I presume. An honor, sir. So kind of you to come. Please have a seat. What can I get you to drink? The service here is a bit—erratic, but I think we will manage somehow." He looked around for the waitress without any conviction.

Gilpin felt as ill at ease as he knew he looked.

"You are no doubt cautious," the fat man continued. "And so you should be. But please rest assured I am an admirer of yours. Oh yes," he said, holding up his right hand as if to swear an oath, "I am very familiar with your writings on the detective genre. It is a hobby of mine.

"One of my many hobbies. Very brilliant your paper on Dorothy Sayers. Deconstructing the mystery novel as either an inherently patriarchal genre that cannot be regendered as a nonsexist narrative, or alternatively as a form of escapist mass literature that presents easy solutions to social problems, thereby expressing the ideology of a dominant group seeking to preserve the status quo by reducing potentially revolutionary social issues to moralistic simplifications of crime and punishment. You see, I am thoroughly conversant. I am not merely attempting ignorant flattery."

"Well, it's really for me just sort of a well, I wouldn't say a hobby, but it's only a minor part of my research. I wrote the Sayers paper and I taught a course last year on detective fiction, but really that's all—look, can't you just tell me what this is all about?"

The fat man laughed, a deep guttural laugh that caused his jowls to shake. "Oh, Professor Gilpin, you academics. The search for the truth. No beating around the bush. No guile, eh?"

Gilpin had the persistent feeling of being the one person at a party who didn't get a joke everyone else was in on. An ageing waitress in a short black cocktail dress and fishnet stockings appeared beside their table. "What can I getcha gentlemen?" she asked, in a tone that implied their existence on the planet was imposition enough without their compounding the affront by expecting to be served a drink on top of it.

"Another diet coke for me," the fat man said, "and for my friend ..." he gestured to Gilpin. Gilpin found himself ordering a brandy; rather to his own surprise.

"Okay, I'll be straightforward because frankly I don't know what else to say," Gilpin said once the waitress had slouched off. "This whole thing is crazy. I mean it's right out of *The Maltese Falcon.* 'G.' And calling me and having me come here to your hotel late at night. And all this mystery about a valuable missing item you're after. And you being, well"—he tried to remember how the fat man had described himself—"corpulent, just like in the story. So what is going on?"

The fat man laughed once again, almost convulsed this time. "Well, I confess I did want to have my little joke. A jeu d'esprit, perhaps one might call it. It did occur to me you would be amused, or at least, I hoped, intrigued. The objective circumstances—here I was looking for something elusive and quite valuable, and my being of a somewhat corpulent build myself, and you being 'tangled' up in this—I couldn't resist adding a few touches from Mr. Hammett's masterpiece. The coincidences just seemed too perfect. And then, with your own métier of searching to construct reality from language, it was a rather delicious fit. You see— reality itself created from the deep structure of the text? Or, as it was rather more quaintly put in my day, 'life imitating art'? But I am quite, quite serious about the manuscript." His eyes narrowed. "Quite serious indeed. I want it. It is mine."

The trio was now assaulting "Night and Day," the guitarist bending every note of the melody into a woozy vibrato while the pianist and drummer banged away, turning the rhythm into an incongruous waltz beat.

"But *why* do you think I know where it is?"

The waitress returned, sloshed their drinks on the table, and stalked away. "My dear sir, you have been as you say 'straight' with me, so I shall be 'straight' with you," the fat man continued. "I don't *know* anything of the kind. But I do know that you are interested in your colleague Professor Glantz's whereabouts. So I have deduced that perhaps you have learned something about *my* manuscript."

"What is this book, anyway? 'Great Jewish Foxhunters.' It sounded like a joke to me."

"You think that, do you?" he said coldly. "That is your professional opinion—as an expert on literature?"

Gilpin sighed and lifted both of his hands impatiently in the air. "I really have no idea."

"Then you really do not know what it is?" the fat man said with a sudden pounce.

"I've told you that. But *you* told *me* you knew where Julie Glantz might be."

"So I did. A slight exaggeration. Perfectly excusable under the circumstances. I do know, however, that in my last conversation with her she was not herself. She had received threats. She was concerned. She was fearful. That is *solid* information, which I give to you as a gift, no strings attached. I do this because it seems eminently plausible to me that he who discovers Professor Julie Glantz's whereabouts will discover the manuscript's whereabouts."

He looked curiously at Gilpin for an instant. "I believe I have read that academics are perpetually discontented? No matter how beautiful the setting, how light the teaching load, how generous the research budgets, they feel—unfulfilled. Dissatisfied. Ill-used. You yourself are still no doubt at that young and idealistic stage of your career, Professor Gilpin, when one is yet immune to such emotions. But I believe I read in this same fascinating article that as academics approach the age of forty they invariably grow bitter and resentful. The students upon whom they have lavished so much hope and idealism prove an ungrateful disappointment. The books they imagined they would write and change the world somehow never quite get written. What they had foreseen to be an idyllic existence surrounded by ideas and likeminded colleagues turns out to be a cesspit of petty politics and monotony.

"And worst of all, there is the galling discovery that all of those none too bright former classmates of theirs who got Cs, and spent their Saturday nights throwing up in the courtyard and endeavoring to ascertain which objects could successfully be set fire to, are now driving Porsches, and already have second wives of unsurpassing attractions half their age who adore them or at least pretend to do so which is much the same thing, and own small islands in Maine or South Carolina where they spend a week here and then when they are not jetting off to Paris or New York or tending to their extremely vast collections of rare vintages.

"And then to add a final insult to injury, these same men of such unquestionably second-rate intellect and unrefined sensibility are rewarded with seats on the boards of trustees of the very institutions of higher learning where they themselves cut such undistinguished careers as undergraduates. Were this a just society, scholars such as yourself think, *you* would be the ones to be so richly remunerated and honored—you who have made the great sacrifices in the pursuit of pure knowledge and the betterment of mankind; you who so indubitably possess the superior intellect and talent. Yet that is most definitely not the case. A strange quirk of our society, but there it is.

"*I* am a very wealthy man, Professor Gilpin. I do not expect to get something for nothing. I can do nothing, alas, about the ingratitude of your students, the pettiness of your colleagues, or the monotony of your teaching duties. But I shall make it worth your while to assist me."

Gilpin had listened expressionlessly to this long speech, and now said nothing when it was done.

"If you learn anything about where Professor Julie Glantz may have taken herself, you *will* let me know, won't you?" the fat man urged. "Of course it is only the manuscript I care about. But means and ends, Professor Gilpin, means and ends. We have different ends, but I believe we may make common cause on the means."

The fat man tossed half of his diet coke down, wiping his mouth with the back of his hand. Gilpin took a cautious sip of his brandy. Its taste reminded him of the smell of jet aircraft fuel.

"This manuscript," asked Gilpin. "Is this something she was writing for you—a sort of private research project?"

"Professor Gilpin, I am a businessman. I learned very early on that one should always maintain the most cordial relations with one's competitors. But I also learned to keep a secret. And the details of this manuscript's origins, and the precise nature of any business relationship I have entered into with Professor Julie Glantz regarding it, must, I am afraid, remain one of those secrets. Suffice it to say, the manuscript is unquestionably mine—morally and legally—mine. That is all that matters for now."

"I'm not even sure it exists."

"Oh, it exists. That is where any superficial resemblance between our little mystery and Mr. Hammett's classic and intriguing novel ends."

"I'd better go. Thanks for the drink. If I do need to get in touch with you, Mr.—"

"No, no names, please. It is better that way. I really am inordinately fond of 'G.' I will, with your permission, check with you from time to time."

Gilpin again gave no assent. Looking unhappy and dissatisfied, he rose. "Until we meet, again Professor Gilpin," the fat man said, holding out his hand. "Happy hunting—as we say. I truly did so admire your article on Dorothy Sayers. Really most admirable. So deserving to become more widely known. Somehow I feel it soon will be. Goodbye."

What the hell did he mean by that, Gilpin thought as he pressed through the revolving door and hunched into his jacket against the bitter lake breeze. He had gone a block before he was sure the whole thing was an elaborate practical joke after all.

He felt his ears blazing with embarrassment in the cold night air. Probably some actor friend of Travis's that he'd put up to it. Nobody talked that way in real life, for chrissake.

And all those references to his own studies of the mystery novel, and that long effort to entice him with visions of wealth into saying something ridiculous and demeaning and mercenary. I mean, that's the essence of a practical joke, isn't it: set someone up so their greed or vanity or gullibility blinds them to even the most obvious warning signs that it's a put-on.

Well, at least he'd kept his mouth shut about that. Hell, the man had even said right out that half of his story was a joke—a nice touch that Travis would no doubt have rubbed in every time he regaled everyone with how vain Gilpin was to have fallen for such a patently ludicrous set up.

A group of boisterous undergraduates, five guys and two girls, reeled past, chanting "Boozeday! Wetday! Thirstday!" and dissolving into uproarious laughter. He tried to remember who had first even brought up the matter of the manuscript and its title. He rather thought the fat man hadn't said anything more than that he was looking for something undefined until Gilpin had mentioned the 'Great Jewish Foxhunters' business. Then when he had pressed him about it, he had just acted knowing and mysterious without committing himself to any details that might have tripped up his story.

Well, even if the fat man had known about it himself that didn't prove anything—anyone could have sent that email to Julie's computer. Though if that had been a prank, too, why hadn't Glantz just deleted it? And Travis could hardly have sent that a week ago to set up this trick tonight. Unless he was playing some joke on Glantz, too. Anyway, there wasn't a scrap of evidence beyond that one email that any such manuscript even existed.

The fat man definitely did know he was looking into Julie Glantz's disappearance. But then everybody seemed to, for God's sake. That also went nowhere. Still, there was that threatening email she had received, and the fat man had spoken of her having received threats. How far would Travis actually go to give credence to a practical joke? Surely he'd draw the line at sending threatening messages.

Gilpin passed the library, its lights blazing through soaring windows, illuminating the bare lawn and sidewalk without, the tables and carrels within deserted and empty: students never even bothered looking anything up in a book anymore, just grabbed whatever assorted garbage they could find on the Internet. The library had taken to desperate measures to entice students through the doors, hoping they might look at, or even check out, a book once inside. They had spent tens of thousands of dollars on extremely comfortable reclining chairs. They had relaxed the rules against eating, drinking, and using cell phones. They had set up a smoking area.

This fall they had advertised a series of promotions, contests, and fun events. Thursdays were now karaoke night at the library; every Saturday at five there was a skateboarding contest down the wide, open, curving stairways that joined the four floors.

Gilpin noticed a few students milling about what looked like a buffet table set up by the reference desk. He paused and squinted through the window at a sign standing on an easel next to the table. MAKE YOUR OWN SUNDAE it read. FREE TO ALL STUDENTS WHO HAVE CHECKED OUT AT LEAST ONE BOOK THIS SEMESTER. PLEASE PRESENT YOUR STUDENT CARD FOR VERIFICATION.

Gilpin arrived home a bit out of breath from his walk. God, I'm getting out of shape, he thought. He glanced at himself in the hall mirror as he passed. His hair was already starting to thin. He was getting a bit of a paunch. Maybe he'd start going to the gym at lunchtime.

He went upstairs to his study, glanced at the emails on his computer, and saw a new message that appeared to have been sent by himself to him. He clicked on it. "YOUR TURN'S COMING, TOO" appeared on the screen. The end of a perfect day. He shut down the computer, went back downstairs to fetch his poetry anthology, hastily got ready for bed, and leafed through the book to find the poem by Norman Cameron that he had been thinking of as he had listened to Anika speak of truth and beauty, and mathematics and music.

He read it once through, barely awake now, then roused himself to reach over and switch off the light on the bedside table, drifting off to sleep with the lines echoing in his fading consciousness:

> *All day my sheep have mingled with yours. They*
> *   strayed*
> *Into your valley seeking a change of ground.*
> *Held and bemused with what they and I had found,*
> *Pastures and wonders, heedlessly I delayed.*

Now it is late. The tracks leading home are steep,
The stars and landmarks in your country are strange.
How can I take my sheep back over the range?
Shepherdess, show me now where I may sleep.

✤ 6.

Like bit players in a vaudeville skit, the students drifted in, singly, at five minute intervals and joined one of the clumps in the rear that formed a steadily growing tableau of studiously posed indifference. Most of them sat slouched sideways at their desks, taking occasional swigs from oversized baby bottles of water or immense coffees; checking email, stock quotes, and poker hands on their laptops; nudging each other from time to time with looks of ironic deprecation. A few merely looked comatose.

Gilpin sat in the front row trying to focus through a dull headache on the student presentations he had scheduled for the first half of his 8:30 a.m. class. They weren't going well. The first year that he had tried to get his class engaged by having the students carry out and report on a "participatory" poetry project they invented themselves, it had been great. One student had somehow worked himself into the good graces of a local Scottish heritage society whose ageing members had enthusiastically adopted him as an honorary member for their weekly malt whisky tastings; the group's entire pipe band, resplendent in kilts and sporans, had marched into class to accompany him as he began reading Burns's "Address to a Haggis":

> *Fair fa' your honest, sonsie face,*
> *Great chieftain o' the pudding-race!*

It had been quite a scene; it had also stirred in Gilpin the vain and rare gratification of a teacher who catches in one of his pupils a glimpse of his own younger self. But for some reason or other the enthusiasm had waned every year since. He didn't know if the students were changing or if he was somehow unconsciously conveying his own creeping loss of innocence and disillusionment as a teacher.

Now some young thing who had a tattoo of what looked like a World War II battleship completely covering her right calf—what was her name, Danielle? Tiffany? he rather thought it was Danielle—was struggling through a Powerpoint presentation reporting on the survey she had done of her four suitemates to whom she had posed the question (according to her title slide) "Is Robert Burn's poems better than sex?" The answer appeared to be no.

"Burns wrote a lot of, like, really expansive poems, so that might be part of why people don't like them," she was saying. "But I found on the Internet a statistic that reading poetry helps keep older minds active, so that could be one useful thing about these poems. That's just my opinion."

Gilpin struggled furiously against a huge yawn and checked his class list; yes, it was Danielle. "Okay, thank you Danielle. That was very—" Gilpin groped for an appropriate word that wouldn't do too much violence to the truth—"creative. Now let's look at the poem you all should be prepared to discuss today, page forty-nine of your anthology..."

The rest of the hour had passed with the usual futile blend of cajolery, flattery, and threats on Gilpin's part and the usual blend of silence, procedural objections, and bored petulance on the students' part.

He walked back to Trojan Hall feeling more defeated than ever. In the end he hadn't dared say much about love or innocence and had confined his remarks about "The Rigs O'Barley" to an analysis of its meter and Burns's role as an enduring working class voice of Scottish nationalism, tying it in finally with the geopoetics of the Glasgow M77 Motorway Protest of 1994.

It had not been Gilpin's best effort, and he knew it.

He had settled wearily into his office chair and was starting to look through his emails when Travis stuck his head in the door and leered. "And what do you think of the latest from our lords and masters?"

"Eric. Tell me the truth. Do you have a friend, very fat, accomplished actor who likes to pretend he's Gutman from *The Maltese Falcon*?"

"Fat? Doesn't sound like anyone I would include in my entourage."

It was impossible to tell from Travis's perennially supercilious expression whether he was ever joking or not, but even though he showed no particular surprise at what would surely have seemed a bizarre question to someone who was innocent of the matter, something in his answer made Gilpin think he was genuinely unwitting of the odd events of the previous night.

"All right, never mind. What latest are you talking about?"

Travis walked over and stood behind Gilpin's shoulder and pointed a few messages down in his email inbox. "elcono adds star power to award-winning faculty" was the subject line.

"ELCONO?" asked Gilpin.

"That is apparently our dear Veep's latest one-word-name brainstorm he's taking out for a spin. I imagine he was inspired by your colloquy yesterday about MIT."

Giplin groaned. He read the rest of the message silently. It announced the hiring of five new adjunct professors, none of whom remotely seemed like "stars" to him, but all of whom were important businessmen or civic leaders in the area, and all of whom were graduates of the university.

"So?"

"Ba-bump, ba-bump, ba-bump. Triple bank-shot."

"Meaning?"

"One, we hire more teachers, increasing the faculty-student ratio, good for the *U.S. News* rankings. Two, we pay them astronomical salaries, increasing average faculty salary, also good for the *U.S. News* rankings. Three, we make them donate most of said astronomical salary back to the university, thereby increasing alumni giving rate, also good for the *U.S. News* rankings. And best of all, we have met all of these lofty academic objectives without costing the university but a fraction of what hiring a real professor would cost. Capiche?"

"But isn't this illegal?"

"Tsk tsk. *Unethical.* Not illegal. *Completely* different thing."

As always, Travis seemed to take unbridled cynical delight in any confirmation that the world at large was every bit as corrupt as one imagined it to be. Gilpin found himself sputtering in outrage, which only added to Travis's pleasure at having been the bearer of the news.

"No use getting your shorts in a twist over it, Teddy boy. Or as Virgil said, cheer up—things could be worse."

"Virgil said that?"

"Well, he actually said, 'Forsan et haec olim meminisse iuvabit'—'Perhaps someday it will be pleasant to remember even this.' Much the same thing, really."

"Do you know Latin?"

"No more than the occasional tag is all that remains, alas, from the reactionary secondary education provided me at minimal charge by the Jesuits. By the way, don't forget to come to my student's performance tomorrow night, will you? The midnight Halloween organ recital? A bit past my own bedtime, I confess. I always prefer to be fully conscious when *experiencing* an *organ* myself"—another totally gratuitous leer—"but I promised him we'd all turn out in solidarity. It's always a lot of fun. Lots of Phantom of the Opera stuff. Boogie-boogie-boogie." He delivered these last words at the door, pausing to turn back and mug a Bela Lugosi pose of hunching his back and raising both hands in clawlike menace.

"Say, Eric."

"Yeeeee-ussssss," he replied, still in Bela Lugosi mode.

"Anika. Is she—I mean, does she, well, live with anyone? Or anything? I mean, do you know?"

"She is married to her work. Her only true passion is the spin state of her electrons. Actually, I have a theory about that..."

"Yes, I know, Eric," Gilpin quickly cut in. "Thanks. See you later."

With a flourish of an imaginary cape, Travis made his exit.

Gilpin thought for a minute, pulled out the sheet on which he'd printed the message out from Glantz's computer, and copied it into an email which he sent to a slight acquaintance in the classics department, asking if he could translate or identify the Latin quotation.

The ringing phone on his desk caused him to jump several inches. He gave the phone a look of deep suspicion and let it ring several more times.

Finally he picked it up like a member of bomb disposal team who, suddenly resigned to his fate, decides to throw caution to the wind. "Hello?"

"Ted, Bob here."

Gilpin exhaled in relief.

"Ted, just touching base with you on the matter we discussed yesterday."

Gilpin waited for him to go on, then realized that this was apparently his cue to speak. "Oh, right. Well, I haven't found out very much yet, to be honest with you. Nobody's seen her since last Friday. There's one, well, strange thing...." He tried to think of how to explain the Great Jewish Foxhunters business. "I don't quite understand it myself, but I think she was working on some sort of odd project and there seem to be some people outside the university involved, but I don't suppose that has anything to with it anyway, so I probably shouldn't have even mentioned it now that I think about it." He realized how idiotic he sounded.

"Ted, glad you mentioned that because I was going to just give you a word of caution. I don't think you need to follow up on the manuscript issue. We've got that in hand on the c-level and it leads into some complicated waters that well, involve the university's finances and some nuances of alumni relations."

"C-level?"

"Right, Ted. I see you get the picture. Knew I could count on you. Keep me in the loop, right? Ted, we'll have to get together for a round of golf sometime."

"Uh, I don't play golf, Bob."

"Well, I can sure understand that, Ted—didn't have as much time for it myself as I wished I did when I was a young go-getter like you. Something to look forward to when you retire, anyway—improving your swing, getting the old handicap down? Well, take care, Ted. Keep me in the loop."

Gilpin typed "C-level" into Google and came up with a reference to "C-level executives," meaning apparently CEO, COO, CFO, and the like.

The phone rang again. He picked it up quickly this time. "Hello, Ted Gilpin here."

"Theodore, thank goodness."

"Mom. Hi."

"You said you would call, and then you didn't, and I tried calling you last night and this morning and couldn't get you."

"Mom—*you* called *me* and we talked for a long time last night. So why would I have still needed to call *you* back after that?"

"Well, you said you would. Maybe you don't remember."

He groaned.

"Yes, I know your mother must be a terrible burden to you, but some day you'll thank me for the tsuris I go through for you. Now, this is what I wanted to tell you. I was watching on 'Oprah,' and there was a policeman who was saying that seventy-two percent—I think it was seventy-two—of all crimes are committed in the workplace. People, they leave their purses on their desks and at lunchtime someone comes and steals them. So, you need to be careful. Maybe you and your friends there should take turns going to lunch so nobody can come in and steal. That's all."

"Okay, thanks mom. I'll, uh, think about, uh—great advice. Good. Thanks."

"So, I don't mean to pry, but how was your date with that girl? She's a nice girl?"

"Mom, it wasn't a 'date.' She's just a colleague. We went and had coffee. Okay?"

"Alright, you don't have to bite your mother's head off. If I can't be interested in my own son, who can I be interested in?"

"Okay, mom, fine. Look, I've got some work to do. Talk to you later."

Chickening out, he sent Anika an email rather than phoning to ask her if she would like to go to the midnight organ concert Friday night. Travis stuck his head back in the door to ask if he'd like to come to lunch, and rewarded him with one of his particularly arch looks when Gilpin said he thought he'd go to the gym instead.

Along with Lawless Chapel and the endowment for the core humanities program, the gym was the other great monument on campus to the founder's largesse. It covered acres of indoor space—lap pools, running track, tennis courts, sauna, weight room, exercise rooms, skating rink, and a separate ice rink just for curling, which had been Evander Lawless's favorite sport, one which, he insisted, promoted peaceful cooperation between nations.

The curling team had always been something of a joke, but last year's team had become so ironically mock-serious about the absurdity of a sport that consisted of one team member sliding a large stone across the ice while the rest of the team furiously swept the path ahead clear with brooms that it had ended up winning the national collegiate championships.

The gym also featured a luxurious bar and lounge, strictly off-limits to students, where uniformed waiters served post-work-out gin and tonics to red-faced faculty members as they sank into redleathered chairs that commanded an odd but strangely calming view through floor-to-ceiling plate glass windows of the nearly always empty curling rink below.

Feeling like an impostor, Gilpin, gym bag in hand, made his way under the gothic arch engraved with the motto MENS SANA IN CORPORE SANO and headed to the locker room to change.

The exercise room was crowded with the usual bifurcated clientele, one part aggressively trim, mostly female, and deadly serious, the devout performing a daily rite; the other part mostly male, paunchy, unconvincing, obvious sinners hoping for quick absolution before returning to the path of backsliding.

Too late, Gilpin saw that the only free exercise bicycle in the entire room was right next to one occupied by his department chairman. Dr. John Doe was wearing a bright yellow Lycra bicycling outfit covered with commercial logos of Tour de France sponsors and was pedaling at a moderate clip while typing on a laptop he had somehow contrived to balance on the handlebars. Doe waved and motioned Gilpin over.

"Ted, hi, uh, here to get some, uh, exercise, eh?"

"Yeah, John."

"Well, great. One of the really nice things here on campus, eh? I mean the gym? And all? Didn't have this back at Iowa. Uh, not that I'm saying anything against Iowa, uh no. Well, Ted, you know one thing I'm really trying to do here is see how we can forge some, uh, interesting collaborations between, uh, cognitive science and the humanities. Great to have this chance to chat with you. Now you take literature. Really just an example of neural networks in action..."

Gilpin found himself pedaling faster and faster as if trying to escape from the stream of jargon bombarding him. He soon was pouring sweat and his calves and stomach were aching, and he abruptly slowed down. He felt a small, burning ember of competitive spirit starting to well up within him and gritted his teeth, determined that he would not be the one to give up first.

Forty minutes later Doe was still going strong, both at the bike and his stream of talk. Gilpin, exhausted, slipped off his bike, mumbled a word of good-bye to Doe, and headed for the showers.

Well, he felt different anyway, he thought as he walked back to his office: his head hurt in a different spot.

A campus police car was parked on the grass by the front of Trojan Hall when he arrived there, just before two o'clock. When Gilpin got to the third floor he heard the crackle of a police radio coming from the end of the corridor. Two large campus cops were standing by the door to his office, looking into the room with seen-it-all expressions on their faces.

"What's the problem, officers?" Gilpin asked as he approached.

"Are you Professor Gilpin?" said the older one, who had a bouncer's build, sergeant's stripes, and brushy iron-gray hair edging his head under his police cap.

Gilpin reached the door and looked in.

The floor was covered with his books. Papers from his file drawers lay in scattered heaps, spilling off his desk. The large cactus was uprooted, the potting soil spilled over his rug. Pictures had been pulled out of their frames and the mats and backings stripped off. The seat of the chairs had been cut open and the stuffing pulled out.

He gazed speechless at the scene.

"Professor, we had a call an hour ago," the cop said. "From someone claiming to be your mother. She said she was concerned your office was going to be robbed. It sounded like a crank call, but we always check these things out. So we came over and found this. Would you happen to know anything about this?"

"I, uh, think it was my mother. I mean who called, not who did this. It's got to be a—crazy coincidence. She, er, reads these articles in supermarket magazines and is always imagining someone is going to rob me. Or tie me up in my office." He felt himself intensely uncomfortable under the blank expressions on the cops' faces. "Or something."

"I see," said the large cop. "Uh-huh. Coincidence. So you don't have any idea who did this?"

"For God's sake, I can't even imagine. I mean, it—was anything stolen?"

"Well, we're hoping you could tell us that. The computer equipment is still here. And a cell phone, it looks like," he said, shifting a pile of papers with his nightstick. "So although I wouldn't want to jump to any hasty conclusions, professor, it has the look of revenge or personal motive rather than theft. Hope you don't mind us asking this, but are you having any trouble with an ex-wife, or girlfriend perhaps?" He glanced at Gilpin and took him in with a quick, encompassing glimpse. "Or other kind of friend?" he added hastily.

"No, I'm not married. And I don't have a girlfriend. I mean right now. I mean of course I have had a girlfriend," he added ridiculously.

"Any students, maybe, with a grudge against you?"

He couldn't imagine they did, since he gave them all As or Bs, no matter how little work they did. "No, I don't think so."

The other cop spoke up. "Professor, several of your colleagues we've spoken to here say you've been asking a lot of questions about one of your colleagues"—he glanced down at his notebook—"Julie Glantz? What's that about, exactly?"

"Well, it doesn't have anything to do with this. I mean, it's just a personal—I mean personnel—matter. I mean the Vice President asked me to find out if anyone had seen her. Because she hasn't been around. Not that she's missing. I'm sure it's just some ordinary thing. Not a police matter," he quickly added.

"So the Vice President asked you to talk to your colleagues?" the younger cop said, exchanging a quick glance with his partner. Each time he said "colleagues," he said it in a way that a person does who has picked up a technical term that he is trying to use to establish his credibility with a member of an in-group, though without knowing exactly what it means.

"Yes, I just told you so."

Again the cops shot a look at one another.

"Well, we know you've been *telling* your colleagues that he asked you to do this."

"Look, why on earth would I make something like that up?"

"Maybe you can tell us."

"Look, this is ridiculous. Somebody trashed *my* office. I'm not the culprit, for chrissake."

"No one suggested you were, professor," the sergeant said re-assuringly. "Now if you could just, as a matter of routine, tell us where you've been the last two hours, so we can file our report and we'll see what we can do."

"I've been at the gym. Dr. Doe can vouch for me if you don't believe me," he said angrily. The younger cop wrote it down. "Look, didn't anybody hear anything?" Gilpin demanded.

"All of your colleagues were at lunch, seems, when it happened," said the young cop. "Except Professor Shalaby. He says he was here but he didn't hear nothing."

"Anything," corrected the sergeant, primly.

"Anything," echoed his partner.

"Professor," the sergeant continued, "we always tell people it's important to leave police matters to the trained professionals. If one of your colleagues is missing, you should file a missing person report and not try to solve things yourself. Now we can't force you to take our advice, but it almost always does more harm than good when civilians try to play cop. Sorry about your trouble here. We'll let you know if we find out anything."

They started to leave.

"Wait a minute, aren't you going to, well, look for fingerprints or something?" Gilpin asked, then immediately feeling foolish and naïve as soon as the words were out of his mouth.

The officers smiled indulgently. "Professor, I'm afraid that's stuff from detective stories," the sergeant said. "Minor act of vandalism, less than $100 property damage, there just isn't that much we can do. In our experience, ninety-nine times out of a hundred, crimes like these are domestics."

The cops rattled off down the hall, radios, handcuffs, holsters, Mace, Tasers, and nightsticks slapping and clanking against their hips as they ambled off.

Gilpin morosely cleared a path to his desk, sat down on the torn office chair, and surveyed the wreckage. He got up, tried to scoop the potting soil back into the large pot, carefully setting the large cactus back in place, which then promptly tipped over. He sat back down and looked at his computer screen. His heart leapt momentarily when he saw an email from Anika: she said she would enjoy going to the concert, would be working late anyway, and perhaps he could come by her office at 11:45 and they would walk over together.

There was also a message from the classics professor, enclosing a translation of the Latin passage:

> *Monsters more fierce offended heaven ne'er sent*
> *From hell's abyss, for human punishment —*
> *With virgin-faces, but with wombs obscene,*
> *Foul paunches, and with ordure still unclean;*
> *With claws for hands, and looks for ever lean.*

He added that it was from Book III of Virgil's Aeneid.

Gilpin was now positive he had seen those lines somewhere before, but still could not think where that might have been.

✤ 7.

It was midmorning Friday before he had finished reshelving his books and getting the worst of the mess back in order—he had been too exhausted and demoralized to do anything about it the day before, and had finally just dragged himself from his chair, shut and locked the door behind him, and taken himself home.

It had not been so easy to shut the door on that compartment of the mind that always seems to brim over with anxious thoughts at 3 a.m. when the more rational components of the brain are somnolent, and after waking from a vague and ill-remembered nightmare he had lain awake for hours tossing and revisiting in his mind's eye the scene of scattered books and the ruined cactus, until at last he had fallen into a deep but all too brief sleep just before dawn.

At seven he had finally gotten up, taken a shower of alternating hot and cold blasts of water, and downed a grandissimo extremo latte from Java Java Java Java on his way in. After about three hours of steady work he had not identified anything definitely missing.

The jolt of caffeine had revived him but left him feeling like a bundle of loose nerve endings. He jumped six inches at the sound of a knock on his open door, banging his knee on the desk drawer in which he was filing away a few student recommendations from four years ago.

"Man, this is getting *ug*-ly." Mfuka was standing at the door shaking his head. "Hell hath *no* motherfucking fury."

"What? Oh, come on, you can't possibly think Wendy trashed my office. Just because you're fighting with her over the dog policy doesn't make her some kind of random psycho office trasher."

"Man, that bitch'll do anything. She's crazy, man, I tell you."

"But why would she do anything to me?"

"She's *crazy*, man," he repeated. Mfuka squinted suspiciously at him. "You been fucking her, man?"

"No, of course not."

"Man, she don't *ever* forgive anybody for that."

"But I just said I *haven't* been doing anything with her."

"Yeah, and *I* just told you that's what she don't forgive."

"Oh." He looked past Mfuka out into the hallway. "Where's Tyrone today?"

"He got group therapy today, man. I tell you, that bitch is *crazy*," Mfuka said, still shaking his head as he walked away.

Hell, Gilpin thought, if it came to crazy, who in the department wasn't.

He spent a few minutes trying to dream up an explanation that could neatly tie together Glantz's disappearance, the fat man, the missing manuscript, the threatening messages, and his trashed office, and got absolutely nowhere.

He pulled out the campus directory, looked up the organ curator's shop in the directory, started to pick up the phone, then abruptly changed his mind, got up, put on his brown tweed jacket, and walked across the quadrangle to Lawless Chapel.

Gilpin went down the dusty basement stairs, past the two huge blowers and associated wiring and huge switches that looked like they were left over from the set of *Frankenstein,* and knocked on the door of the organ shop.

A pleasant young female voice called to him to come in. A plain but trim girl in blue jeans and a shop apron, her long black hair in a neat ponytail, was looking with professional contempt at the parts of an ancient drill press spread out on the bench in front of her. She grinned sardonically at Gilpin's look of curiosity. "Joe

Dwight's Second Law: everything was better in the old days. Of course *he* never has to try drilling a hole with this piece of crap."

The walls of the shop were lined with shelves of dusty bottles and cans bearing advertising logos from the first half of the twentieth century, filled with washers and springs and other less recognizable small parts.

Old framed pictures of men in tails seated at the organ; a large panoramic view of a group at a picnic, all in coats and ties, the women carrying parasols; old posters for concerts filled the few remaining spaces on the wall. Gilpin looked around and then back at the drill press.

"That's quite an antique."

"Yeah, since Joe found that old picture of the shop from the 1930s that had this same drill press in it," she said, pointing to one of the pictures on the wall, "he started insisting we could never replace it—because it was part of our 'heritage.'"

"I like old hand tools myself, but I'm not sure I could feel much nostalgia for that."

"Yeah, well this is the last time I'm messing with it. We're about to give Joe an ultimatum—the drill press goes or we go. Though now that I hear myself saying it, maybe that isn't such a smart choice to offer somebody like him."

"Is Joe around?"

"Yes, he's upstairs doing some tuning and adjustments for the concert tonight. Is there something you needed?"

"Well, I'm Ted Gilpin—from the D-CADS department. I was just wondering if he might have a few minutes to show me around the organ. But if he's busy—"

"Oh I'm sure he wouldn't mind. You can just go on up. Up the side stairs to the balcony and the door should be open there."

"Thanks."

"You'd better take these," she said tossing him a pair of extremely heavy-duty hearing protectors, the kind that jet-aircraft maintenance men and rifle-range instructors wear. "He's going to be tuning the 32' bombarde in a minute and if you're back there when they're sounding they'll blow your eardrums out. Here's a sheet on the history of the organ you can have, too."

Gilpin followed her directions to the organ chamber. It was an eerie, cavernous space tucked high above and behind the stage of the chapel, so perfectly concealed in the building's architecture that no one sitting below would even guess of its existence had they not known it was there.

As he walked through the door a narrow path squeezed its way between a forest of metal and wooden pipes. The ones by the door were easily three stories tall and as big around as a sewer main. It was like an industrial fantasy of a cavern. Overhead, by the glimmer of a faint work light, Gilpin made out a series of ladders and stairways climbing into a shadowy gloom. "Hello?" he called out. "Your assistant told me to come up."

"Hello," a cheery voice called back. "Up the main ladder, then along the catwalk and up the next ladder and on through the small doorway right in front of you. I'm back here in the solo division. If heights bother you don't look down. And if you fall and land on any of the pipes, you better hope the fall kills you—because if it doesn't, I will."

Gilpin was once again struck by how much happier people who managed to find a way of combining work with their hands and their minds always seemed to be. They were always straightforwardly confident; even their gripes and complaints had a fresh and direct character that stood in such marked contrast to the catty and repressed petulance of academics. He mused about the artisan's sources of contentment: confident possession of expert knowledge; a clear purpose to apply it to; a tangible result you could see and touch.

Well, scholars didn't used to be that terribly different. Find some patient and modest task, like a translation or editing a collection of letters, or tracing historical references in an important literary work, and set to it. It used to be that the highest compliment you could pay a scholar was to say that he was "sound." Now everyone had to be "smart" or "daring" or "transgressive"—the relentless push to break rules and boundaries, to thumb your nose at the very definition of traditional scholarship, to be a creative badboy rather than solid and practical.

He thought of Bach, Beethoven, Van Gogh, Picasso; well, creative geniuses usually did break down barriers, but breaking down barriers didn't automatically make one a creative genius. Usually it just made one a sophomoric prick. Education and expert knowledge didn't make a person creative in and of themselves, that was for sure.

And how many creative geniuses could the world ever produce? Not enough to fill the humanities departments of a thousand American universities, *that* was for sure. Maybe that's why we all act all like a bunch of prima donnas, Gilpin thought. No man has more arrogance than a bad poet—except maybe one who looks himself in the mirror in the morning while he's shaving and knows he's bad.

He reached the top of the second ladder and then had to simultaneously turn sideways and stoop to squeeze through the door that led to the enclosed chamber where the curator was working.

The room, about thirty by thirty feet, was impossibly crammed with pipes of all sizes. Two massive shutters along the front wall were partially open, offering a dizzying glimpse of the floor of the hall far below. The sense of being a cave explorer in a surrealistic techno-world intensified.

"Be with you in a second!" a voice called down.

Gilpin looked up and saw a form leaning out precariously from a catwalk several dozen feet above and lowering what appeared to be a grappling hook on a coiled rope down the gaping opening of one of the monster pipes. He tried several more casts and then slowly began pulling the rope up.

A minute later Joe Dwight was down the ladder, standing beside Gilpin, displaying his catch, which appeared to be a significantly decomposed bat. "One of the organists left a note that the low D on the 32' bombarde was out, and here's the culprit," he said with an air of small triumph. "This whole column of air vibrates at 16 cycles per second, and the force is obviously powerful enough to just have sucked that bat right in. It was really jammed in there."

Gilpin introduced himself and explained that he was hoping to have a look around the organ. "Well, help yourself. Just be careful on the catwalks and don't start grabbing at the pipes to balance yourself. I'd be happy to show you around but I've got the tuning to finish."

"You know, I think maybe one of the other members of my department came by last week to have a look at the organ—Julie Glantz?"

"No. No, I don't think so." He shook his head.

"She didn't call you?"

"No, name doesn't ring any bells."

The curator had been fiddling with a rubber tube at the base of the pipe from which he had extracted the bat when suddenly a deafening blast struck Gilpin's ears. It was a physical blow, staggering, accompanied by the sensation of the entire room pressing in from all sides. In the small enclosed chamber the sound seemed to be coming from everywhere, almost from inside of himself. It was an intensely painful but also claustrophobia-inducing feeling: he literally felt he couldn't breath for a few seconds against the encircling pressure.

Dwight hastily yanked the tube out. "Sorry about that. Ciphering—stuck note. I'm embarrassed to say I wasn't expecting or even thinking of that as a possibility once I solved the bat problem."

"God, that was—unnerving."

"Yeah, it'll put the fear of God in you," he agreed, grinning like a schoolboy who had just set off a particularly satisfying explosion with his chemistry set.

Dwight deftly unscrewed a dozen screws from the bottom of the wind chest and plucked out a small circle of leather-covered wood that had come loose from a dowel. He showed Gilpin the defective part and explained the mechanism: a series of cascading pneumatic chambers carved out of wooden channels, regulated by leather valves, acted as a pneumatic amplifier, translating a tiny imbalance in air pressure triggered by an electric solenoid into increasing large flows of air that finally sent a roar of pressurized air into the huge pipes.

A Victorian Rube Goldberg machine—except, Dwight was saying, that it worked more perfectly than anything devised since; the amplification occurred almost instantaneously, a press of the keyboard three hundred feet away causing a note to speak without the slightest detectable delay.

"Better put those on in case I pull another bone-headed move," Dwight said jauntily, indicating the ear protectors, as he began to reassemble the chest.

Gilpin, still a bit shaken, his ears still ringing, thanked him, put on the ear protectors, and cautiously began picking his way around the rest of the organ chambers.

He had no idea what he was looking for, if anything. He glanced down at the information sheet the curator's assistant had handed him. The Lawless Organ, it was clear, was another one of those white elephants from the period of the college's founding that survived as a quirk of history and the founding family's largesse.

An immense electromechanical marvel of the late nineteenth century—12,000 pipes, one of the largest instruments of its day, miles of wire and tens of thousands of pneumatic valves: high culture brought to the edge of the prairie courtesy of American mechanical ingenuity. The idea was apparently that in a day when symphony orchestras were scarce, great organs like this would provide the next best thing, reproducing the sounds of strings, flutes, and reeds with their ranks upon ranks of pipes. Visiting organists performed transcriptions of symphonic warhorses—the *Ride of the Valkyries*, the *Pomp and Circumstance* march, Handel's Largo; and all of the local Midwestern rubes had packed the chapel for those concerts to prove how cultured they could be.

The instrument had fallen into disfavor with the rise of the authentic-instrument movement of the late twentieth century, and transcriptions had fallen out of fashion. The university nonetheless still spent tens of thousands of dollars a year maintaining the Lawless Chapel organ in obedience to the terms of the bequest.

Aside from the one deliberately campy Halloween concert, the organ was used mainly for the convocation and commencement ceremonies each year and a couple of token and sparsely attended church services that still took place in the chapel. Still, there was something to be said for quaint tradition in a university, Gilpin thought. The only thing holding back the bottom-line Philistinism of the Welches of the modern world, who wanted to turn universities into models of corporate efficiency.

Well, thank God for inefficiency sometimes.

He began to hear—mostly feel—the rumble of the low pipes being tuned, picked his way carefully down the ladders and out, stopping in the basement to return the hearing protectors.

"Did you see what you came for?" the girl in the organ shop asked him. She had the drill press back together but was still wrinkling her nose at it like it was a fish that had been sitting around unrefrigerated for a week.

"Yes—thanks. Well, actually, there is something else I wondered about. Did another professor in my department, Julie Glantz is her name, call you or come by to see the organ last week?"

"No, I don't think so. I'm sure I would have remembered."

"Is the door up there usually locked?"

"Yes. Well, it's sometimes open if we're coming and going during the day doing some work up there. But then we usually have an eye on it so nobody can just wander in."

"Okay. Well, thanks again." He looked with a sudden stab of envy at the pieces of beautifully shellacked knotless pine sitting on her bench, some section of the organ being overhauled with its perfectly spaced rows of holes and neat strips of felt and white leather that were in the process of being glued to the edges.

"It must be—well, very satisfying, the work you do." He immediately regretted his words, realizing how patronizing they must have sounded, but the girl's deadpan expression gave way to a slight hint of something that looked more like cynical amusement than offense.

"You sound like Joe. He's always talking about the 'psychic rewards' of the job. That's a fancy way of saying the pay stinks."

Gilpin, embarrassed still, laughed and said, "Okay, sorry about that. Thanks again."

"No problem."

Gilpin spent his lunch hour again at the gym, swimming desultory laps without very much conviction but at least succeeding in evading Dr. John Doe this time. He was back at Trojan Hall in time for D-CADS department meeting that Doe had summoned for two o'clock. It was probably not the wisest of moves to schedule a meeting for that time on a Friday; the air of the conference room was equal parts gin fumes and belligerence.

Dr. John Doe sat at the head of the table; Gilpin sat down next to Travis as he usually did but then noticed that the remaining three members of the department had spread themselves as far apart as possible from one another around the long table. Dr. John Doe had barely finished saying "Uh, well, okay, uh, let's begin" when Shalaby interrupted, practically trembling with fury.

"I demand an immediate investigation of the McCarthyite witch hunt being conducted on this campus against a scholar whose 'crime' is that he is the greatest academic danger to the imperialist myths of American virtue in the Middle East."

Dr. John Doe looked confused.

Heatherton gave Shalaby a glance of undisguised contempt.

Travis began softly whistling "Hi Ho, Hi Ho, It's Off to Work We Go." Bariki said mildly, "Hey, man, we all got bullshit to put up with."

"You call this bullshit? This is not bullshit. I know bullshit. *This* is an effort to silence the voices that expose the Zionist and imperialist hegemony in what passes for contemporary American intellectual thought. Listen to this: 'Go back to Arab lands where Jew hating is condoned. You are a typical pathetic Arab liar.'" The sheet he was reading from was shaking in his hand.

"Uh, Douad, uh, what is that you're reading there?" asked Dr. John Doe.

"This is a typical example of the anonymous hate mail I have been receiving over the last few days. It comes from somewhere within the campus. I demand an investigation of this right-wing attempt to silence and chill academic freedom of speech in the classroom."

"Actually, I got one, too," said Travis off-handedly. Gilpin, catching that tone, gave him a quick look. Travis had a way of acting the mildest when he was about to become the most mercilessly goading. He had an unerring ability to put his finger on a sore spot; the more he pressed, the more innocent he would act. It usually happened when he'd more than his usual quota of a single martini at lunch.

"The one I got actually made some interesting allusions to some inside details concerning department finances," Travis went on, raising his eyebrows. "It does seem to me that whoever's sending these billet-doux shows a certain skill in knowing just where the *buttons* are we each have. Little hidden anxieties about our temperament"—he looked with total innocence at Shalaby—"or our collegiality"—the same look at Bariki—"or our *sexual* rivalries"—he glanced at Heatherton—"or our scholarly gravitas"—turning finally to Gilpin.

"As a matter of fact," said Heatherton after a long pause, "I did get one of these hate messages, too."

"What, only one, man?" muttered Bariki.

"What's that supposed to mean?" she snapped.

"Uh, well, what did, uh your message, say?" Dr. John Doe intervened hastily.

"I am *not* going to read it out before *this* group. But it was obviously written by someone *very* familiar with the department." She glared at Shalaby, Bariki, Travis, and Gilpin in turn.

Dr. John Doe looked more perplexed than worried. "Uh, gee, well, did anyone else get one of these? Mfuka?"

"Yeah, man. Some bullshit about my dog." He stared menacingly at Heatherton in turn.

"If you're suggesting I sent it, I demand that you retract that," Heatherton said. "And *I* wouldn't be surprised in any case if whoever is sending these sent one to himself—just to cover his tracks."

"Or to *her* fucking self to cover *her* fucking tracks," Bariki said in a mocking sing-song.

"Well, people who display a contempt for *any* of the shared values of the community can legitimately expect to have questions raised as to their respect for *other* shared values as well," Heatherton shot back.

"Uh, okay, well, okay," said Dr. John Doe ineffectually. He turned to Gilpin. "Uh, Ted, did you get, uh, one of these? And, by the way, sorry to hear about what happened to, uh, your office there, Ted."

"Yes, I got one. It just said, 'your turn's coming.' That was last night, before my office was broken into. The funny thing was that the message looked like I had sent it myself." Everyone looked at him. "I mean, I didn't, of course."

"In *fairness*," Heatherton added, "I will say that my first thought about the message I received was—to be completely honest—that it came from Julie." There was an awkward silence. "It used some—phrases—that she herself had used before. I know that may sound strange. But she certainly has been exhibiting definite signs of paranoia lately. We need to face up to facts. And now she's disappeared, after all. Clear sign of paranoid tendencies."

"Man, now we got a fucking psychiatrist on call in addition to an expert on multiple fucking chemical sensitivity disorder," Bariki said, shaking his head.

"Well, maybe our boy detective here," Heatherton said, jabbing a thumb toward Gilpin in a gesture that seemed to redirect all of her anger from Bariki to him, "can tell us what he's found out about Julie. Because if she—or anyone else—is experiencing some mental health changes that are expressing themselves in the acting out of threats, I think we need to consider our personal health and safety and insist that the university administration provide us appropriate support. The administration cannot evade its responsibility for the hostile atmosphere that its own policies help create."

"Actually, I think Julie had received some of these threatening messages herself," Gilpin said. "Before she disappeared."

"That doesn't prove anything," said Heatherton. "As I said, anyone could have sent them. She could have sent them herself— that would be typical of someone exhibiting signs of paranoia."

"What *was* that message about that you got?" Travis asked Heatherton, his tone and facial expression as painstakingly neutral as before.

"About—who—had—the biggest—*balls*—in the department," she said, enunciating each word clinically and precisely. "I mean that metaphorically."

"Yeah, or who's the biggest ball *buster,*" said Bariki.

"I am going to report that remark to the Committee on Gender Sensitivity and Sexual Harassment," Heatherton retorted furiously, at which Shalaby, Heatherton, and Bariki all began talking at once. Travis's expression became more saintlike than ever. Dr. John Doe tried without any visible success to restore order.

"You know something, don't you?" Gilpin murmured to Travis as the words continued to fly across the table around them. "You were trying to draw everyone out, weren't you?"

Travis said nothing. Heatherton stormed out of the room, followed by Shalaby. Bariki said something about having to get his dog, and stalked off contemptuously. Dr. John Doe blinked a few times and said, "Well, uh, I'd wanted to talk about, uh, cognitive science, but, I guess we'll, uh, wait 'til next time. Have a nice, uh, weekend."

Gilpin got up sheepishly, feeling deeply embarrassed by the scene he had just witnessed; Travis, by contrast, had the air of a man rising from a table after a particularly satisfying meal.

"Come on, Eric—what's up?" Gilpin tried again as they reached the corridor. But he was met only with a wan smile that the sphinx himself could have envied.

✜ 8.

Ted and Anika sat in the balcony, looking down on a sea of costumed students. He had counted six George W. Bushes, eight Michael Jacksons, and three Donald Trumps so far; he had lost count of French maids, some of whom, as Eric Travis would have said, could have given a corpse an erection. A raft of black and orange helium balloons floated over the audience, and a steady roar of drunken shouts of friends calling to each other and stage shrieks and fiendish laughs rose up from below.

He had started to tell Anika about the strange doings in his department when the tolling of the bell from the chapel tower interrupted. On exactly the twelfth stroke, the lights melodramatically went out and the organist, in full Dracula garb, made a grand entrance from the side door, illuminated by a single shaft of light from a traveling spotlight. Tumultuous applause and whistles.

With a sweep of his cape he sat down at the console, and had not even touched the seat when the trill and descending minor scale in stark open parallel octaves, the famous opening flourish of Bach's D minor Toccata and Fugue, reverberated through the hall. Three descending figures, each with its dramatic pause to allow the sound to echo and fade away, then the bone-rattling low D from the pedal and the slow build up of the immense chord.

Gilpin recognized the 32' bombarde shaking under it all; it was almost painfully loud even from where they were sitting back in the balcony. He felt a small chill down his spine thinking what that full chord would sound like within the organ chamber.

The toccata continued its familiar course, flights of phantasmic melody alternating with the lumbering minor chords, always underpinned by the steady downward march of fortissimo pedal notes; then the single high note once again emerging by itself from the thundering chord to carry on with another nightmarish run of fancy.

Then at last the resolution coming with a suddenly purposeful harmonic and rhythmic movement replacing the episodic bursts; and then the fugue emerging seamlessly out of it, its theme built from the same descending minor scale that had opened the toccata.

During the fugue several of the Michael Jacksons got up from their seats and started moonwalking in the aisles to the cheers of their friends. Then the final improvisational coda with all the stops pulled literally setting the windows rattling, and so on to the final D minor cadence, which the organist shamelessly milked for all it was worth. The students stood up, hooting and clapping.

Ted scanned the audience during the applause. "I wonder where Eric is. Have you spotted him?"

"No, I haven't seen him yet either."

"Oh well, I'm sure he's here somewhere. Probably disguised as a drag queen with a feather boa, knowing him," he said as a student in just such an outfit walked by and took a seat a few rows behind them next to an Amazon and a Frankenstein's monster complete with bolts sticking out of his neck. "I wonder what J. S. Bach would think of this."

"I think he would approve," said Anika. "You know, in Europe we are always so serious about classical music, but you would never have this many students come to an organ concert. And I think they are actually into it in a way—the music."

The program was, from a strictly musical point of view, bizarre, but the organist clearly knew his audience and the occasion, and the rest of the concert was equally a success. A soft and very eerie movement from a Mendelssohn organ sonata followed, a muffled melancholy reed winding its way through the almost oriental-sounding melody as it traced the intervals of a harmonic minor scale to a muted gravissimo accompaniment.

What was it Charles Rosen had called Mendelssohn—the inventor of religious kitsch. Music that didn't really express anything, merely left the listener with the illusion of having been present at a religious service. Casting an aura of pious devotion without making any awkward demands. Well, so what: great are the uses of bad art at times.

Next came a lavish orchestral transcription of an excerpt from *Sheherazade.* More kitsch but quite magnificent, the sounds of the orchestral parts seeming to emerge from every direction, and then one electrifying moment there in the darkened hall when the distant shimmering of the massed chorus of pipes that evoked the sound of orchestral strings kaleidoscopically swelled into a sweeping tidal wave of sound, the full organ filling every corner of the space.

The uses of bad art indeed, for Ted found he had taken Anika's hand at that moment. He seemed much more surprised than she was; actually, she didn't seem surprised at all, but he could not quite believe he had done that. But so they had sat through the rest of the piece holding hands in the dark.

Then the lights had come up and the students had begun whistling and cheering again and they had separated their hands to join the applause and the spell was broken, and they had chatted for a moment about music, he self-consciously striving to sound natural, she by all appearances perfectly so.

The last piece on the program was another transcription, *The Sorcerer's Apprentice,* which quite brought the house down. The organist bowed with many flourishes of his cape, and the students began drifting boisterously out into the night. Ted and Anika made their way down to the small knot that had gathered around the organ console congratulating the organist, and introduced themselves as friends of Travis's. "By the way, it's strange I haven't seen him yet," Gilpin mentioned. "Do you know where he is?"

The organist said he didn't, and they had started to talk about the organ and the program when the organist excused himself for a second and turned to speak to Joe Dwight, who had just joined the group. "Joe, the 32' bombarde is out again. It was working at the beginning of the Bach but then I lost it almost right away and I had to pull another couple of pedal reeds to cover it up. I hate to bother you with this right now but we've got that master class coming in first thing tomorrow morning."

Ted recognized the girl from the organ shop, in a French maid's costume, standing with some friends a few rows back. Dwight pulled a few stop levers in and out and tried a few notes then called over to her, "Sarah, would you mind running up and checking the sharp side of the bombarde right now? Maybe it's something easy and we can take care of it right away."

The girl slipped off her very high black heels and gamely padded off in stocking feet to the balcony. She was back a few minutes later. "Joe, have you got the key to the inner door of the solo division? It's locked for some reason."

"That's strange," Dwight said. "I always leave it unlocked. Oh well, premature Alzheimer's strikes every fifteen minutes." He pulled out a ring of keys from his pocket and tossed them to her.

Everyone had been hearing blood-curdling screams from girls all night, so one more high-pitched shout made little impression at first. Gilpin was the first to realize something was wrong: it wasn't a stage shriek, but a voice calling insistently for help, its timbre modulated by urgency rather than theatrics. Then it came more loudly and clearly, from just behind the open lattice high on the left side above the stage. "Could someone come up here and help, please. And call an ambulance."

Gilpin and Dwight ran for the stairs. Anika called after them, "I'll call," and pulled out her cell phone.

At the door of the organ chamber Dwight paused for an instant to hit a bank of switches and three stories of lights came on, catwalks and pipework materializing out of the gloom. Up the large ladder, across the catwalk, up the dizzying second ladder, actually more frightening with the view below so well illuminated this time, through the small door to the solo division: and there was a scene out of a campy French farce, a girl in a maid's uniform bending over a form decked out in frilly dress with huge stuffed bosom, blue wig, feathered boa, and rhinestone glasses.

Except that Eric Travis, whose face was approximately the same shade as his wig, was quite unmistakably dead, dead to a certainty that no actor or Hollywood makeup artist could simulate.

A steady hiss of air was coming from the supply duct he had fallen against, dislodging it from the air chest that held the huge pipes. His hands were clenched rigidly over his ears. Gilpin had rushed forward, then halted when he saw the frozen look on Travis's face, then had bent down and gently touched the lifeless arms. They were absolutely, grotesquely rigid. More grotesque was the expression on Travis's face: for it was one of pure, unmitigated terror.

Dwight was gently helping his assistant to her feet and suggesting they go outside and get some air, reassuring her that the EMTs would be there in a minute. He and Gilpin exchanged a brief look of futility, pain, and resignation. Gilpin started to follow the other two out, but an atavistic sense of the impropriety of leaving the dead unattended overcame him, and he turned back and stood over the body for a minute.

It was then that he noticed the piece of plain white paper, folded in quarters, lying next to the right side of Travis's head. It was partially beneath the hand that was clasped over the right ear.

Gilpin hesitated, reached for it, and found the corner was in fact clutched tightly in Travis's right hand. He pulled a little harder but the grasp was absolute iron.

The squawk of a radio and the rattle of metallic equipment came from below. Gilpin finally gave the paper a firm jerk, leaving the torn corner behind. He unfolded it. It was a print-out of what looked by its format to be an email message, but missing the header and subject line. "I know what you're doing and you really can't," was printed at the top. Below that, with a vertical line running along the left margin indicating that it was text forwarded or pasted from another message, was a passage in Latin. Gilpin instantly recognized the words that began it: *tristius haud illis monstrum.*

He also at that moment knew with absolute certainty where he had seen those words the first time. It was the poison-pen message, left pinned with a bread-knife to the torso of the effigy of a female don, in Dorothy Sayers's novel *Gaudy Night.* And he realized that the reason he knew that was because the circumstances of Eric Travis's death had followed, with a precision that could have been scripted, the central plot of another of Dorothy Sayers's novels, *The Nine Tailors.*

The EMTs sidled into the organ chamber with their usual professional air of unconcern. Why the hell didn't they ever hurry, Gilpin wondered. Not that it made any difference now, but they couldn't know that. Gilpin stood aside while one of the technicians felt for a pulse, drew out a stethescope and listened perfunctorily, and got on his radio. "We've got a 10-55 here." He turned to Gilpin. "What do you call this place?"

"Uh, the organ chamber."

"In the organ chamber, off the balcony in the chapel...yeah, 10-45D...no, D as in dead." He gave a grimace of a smile. "Roger."

He turned again to Gilpin. "You'd better leave this to us, now, sir. We need to have the M.E. come in and nothing should be disturbed."

He didn't know why, but Gilpin slid the sheet of paper surreptitiously into his pocket.

From the stunned faces of the group still gathered around the organ console, Gilpin figured Dwight had already broken the news to them. Sarah the assistant curator sat in a seat in the first row nearby, looking stoical but shaken; Dwight stood next to her looking concerned but a bit helpless. Anika came up to Ted and gently laid her hand on his forearm for a few seconds. The two campus cops whom Gilpin recognized from his encounter with them at his office that morning came down the aisle of the hall talking into their radios. They glanced around at the group.

"I understand you found the body?" the sergeant said to Gilpin.

"No, I guess I was the second one there. She was actually the first on the scene," Gilpin said, discreetly indicating Sarah with a glance of his eyes.

"Who made the 911 call?"

"That was me. I," said Anika.

"Uh huh. Okay, we'll need to have a statement from all of you," he said, motioning to the three of them. "If you'll just have a seat and please don't speak to one another until we've had a chance to talk to you each first. Just routine, you understand. But just sit in separate rows, if you would. We'll try to have you out of here as fast as we can."

Gilpin raised his eyes apologetically to Anika and took a seat in the row behind her. The cops had a brief word with the others who had been standing around the organ console, sent a few out of the hall and had the organist and Dwight take a seat with them. Gilpin suddenly felt as drained as he could ever remember feeling in his life. He let his eyes rest on the graceful outline of Anika's neck and the soft fall of her hair; it gave him the sensation of sinking into a cool pool on a torpid day, soothing rather than arousing in his exhaustion.

It was close to two in the morning when the sergeant came up to him, the last to be interviewed. The others had been interviewed and gone home; Anika had spoken briefly to the sergeant and had then said she would wait for him.

"Would you just come with me for a minute, professor?" The cop led him once again back up the now-familiar route to the organ chamber, and then the climb up the ladders to where Travis's body still lay.

A middle aged man with an unkempt beard, wearing notably less than clean surgical scrubs over his blue jeans, was sitting on the floor next to the body, a black medical bag open in front of him. The other cop stood by placidly observing the proceedings. A photographer was packing up his gear. The sergeant nodded to them as he entered.

The examiner was in the process of cutting a slit in the dress as they came in. He stopped and spoke over his shoulder.

"Hey, sarge, don't you bozos know a body is mine? Who's been messing with it?"

The sergeant grunted. The examiner went back to his work. Taking a small knife, he plunged it with frightening force directly into the abdomen of the corpse, through the slit he had cut in the clothing. He then extracted a ten-inch long probe from the bag and jabbed it into the wound he had just made. Gilpin felt himself turn white. The cop grabbed his arm to steady him, eyeing him closely.

"Don't know why we even bother doing this any more," the medical examiner was now saying jauntily, to no one in particular. "All the data relating body temperature to time of death is pure hooey. And you got to get all the way into the liver to get a good reading."

Gilpin saw the room fade into black and white. His vision narrowed and he realized he was about to faint. "I think I'll just sit down here for a second," he said weakly. He put his head between his knees and slowly felt the blood returning as the examiner went on with his monologue.

"Thirty-three point two Celsius," the examiner was now saying, reading the thermometer, "—doesn't mean a damned thing. Obvious shock, thin clothing, large contact area with a cold surface. All would decrease temperature anyway. Could just as easily have happened half an hour ago. Which we know it didn't. I suppose you've been wondering about the rigor." The examiner turned his head and looked over at Gilpin for the first time.

"Me?" said Gilpin. "I did notice his arms and hands were stiff—like iron."

"Yup, well normally rigor mortis sets in several hours after death. Of course there's so much variation that estimating time of death from rigor is a lot of hooey, too. But sometimes, in cases of violent death or intense emotional shock, the muscles of the hands and forearms become completely rigid at the very instant of death. Cadaveric spasm. You sometimes find a weapon clutched in the hand of a victim. Literally impossible to unclasp the hand and remove it. Interesting here the victim was holding a piece of paper that seems to have been torn from his hand. Does suggest a struggle. Though I'd say the proximate cause of death was certainly sudden cardiac arrest. Was there a history of heart disease?"

"Geez, not that I ever knew. Though I doubt he would have told me if there was. He was, well, rather vain about his health. And looks."

"So I see," the examiner said with cheery sarcasm, running his eyes over the ornate costume the body was clad in.

"I mean, what kind of heart disease?" Gilpin asked.

"Of, could be coronary atherosclerosis, aortic valvular stenosis, certain heart arrhythmias."

"Are these things a person would even know he had?"

"Oh, possibly. Though sometimes they're asymptomatic—until you're dead, that is. Which is a rather a dramatic symptom if you think about it. Well, we'll just try flexing a few of these other joints to complete the picture." Gilpin felt a surge of heat flush back over him.

"Okay," the sergeant said to him, "let's go have a talk now, professor."

Propping him up by the arm once again, the sergeant led him out of the room, beckoning his partner to follow. "Maybe you want to just catch your breath here while we ask you a few questions. I'm not sure you want to be climbing on ladders right this second, right?"

They were standing on one of the narrow catwalks and Gilpin felt far from sure of his balance, but it was undeniably better than trying to negotiate the ladders until he felt steadier.

"Now, the way it looks, professor, either Professor Travis accidentally managed to get himself trapped in here or someone deliberately locked him in. Maybe a practical joke that got out of hand. And the shock of the sound triggered a heart attack. You know, professor, I used to be on homicide downtown with the city police before I got this nice job at the university. Cops like me and doc there are used to gory details. But you know, as you happened to see just now, it's a pretty gruesome business, no way around it. Death.

"Now what I was wondering, professor, is why exactly you were looking around this place this afternoon? Both Mr. Dwight and Ms. Battell confirm that. A bit unusual for someone in your line, isn't it? You're not a music professor, are you, professor?"

"No of course not. I—I don't really know what I was looking for. Well, I saw that Julie Glantz had been planning to take a tour of the organ before she disappeared last week, and I just thought that well there might be some, well, clue or something." He realized how hollow it sounded.

"Uh huh. Now professor, you remember what I mentioned to you this morning? About amateurs getting involved in things where they don't have the professional training. Let me give you an example. You see, you teach classes. Now, I wouldn't try to do that. So you see, I'm saying maybe you just better leave this to us."

Gilpin said nothing. "How did you learn that Professor Glantz had taken a tour of the organ?" the sergeant continued.

"Well, I don't think she actually did. Look, there's something else I wanted to mention." He pulled the folded paper from his pocket. "I was the one who took this out of *his* hand," he said, gesturing to the direction of the enclosed chamber. "After we found him in there. And I'll tell you that Julie Glantz received the exact same message last week, too. She'd been getting threats. So I think it does look like something really bad is going on here."

"When did you last see Professor Travis?"

"This afternoon, at our department meeting. I was expecting to see him at the concert, but..."

"When was the last time you were back here?"

"This morning. Look, you can't possibly think I had anything to do with this."

The sergeant looked at the sheet. "Is this Latin?"

"Yes, that's right."

"Why did you take this? Didn't you realize you shouldn't disturb anything at a crime scene?"

"Well, I hardly knew it was a crime scene at that point. And, I was just meaning to look at it. But when I saw that it was the same message Julie received, it sort of well, froze me. I mean of course I was intending to turn it over to the police first chance I had."

"Uh huh." The sergeant stared at the paper some more. "Can you read this?"

"No, I don't know Latin. But I did get a translation. I mean of the note Julie got. Which is the same. It has to do with harpies."

"Harpies?"

"Mythological creatures. Monsters—the head and body of a woman, but wings and tail and talons of a bird. Foul creatures that wallow in ordure."

"Ordure. That's a new word on me, professor. But I like to collect words. What's it mean, exactly?"

"Uh, filth, excrement, that sort of thing."

"Ordure. That's good." He nodded his head in approval. "And just how, professor," continued the sergeant, "did you happen to see this note Professor Glantz got? And you never answered me either about how you knew she was interested in touring the organ last week."

"Well, as I told you, the Vice President asked me just informally to ask if anyone knew where Julie had gone. And, well, her office was open and so I looked just around there. A bit. I mean that's all."

The sergeant sighed. "You know, professor, you may not think we cops have a very hard job. I mean compared to yours. I'm sure you don't think that it's intellectually very challenging and all. But let me tell you a few things that don't add up to me. And like I say, maybe they don't add up because I'm not smart enough to do the adding. But first you go around asking a lot of questions about Professor Glantz. Okay. Then you go for a tour of the organ, and again you ask all kinds of questions about Professor Glantz. Then you take a note from the deceased and again you say there's a connection to Professor Glantz. Now you seem to be going to an awful lot of trouble to let everyone know that some unusual things you're doing the last couple of days are all because you're looking into the whereabouts of Professor Glantz."

"But they are. I told you. The Vice President asked me to do this."

"Yeah, well that's the problem I have making this add up. *You* say he asked you to do this. That's not what he says."

"What?"

"That's what he said, professor," the second cop confirmed.

"You sure you don't want to think this over and tell it to us from the beginning?" said the sergeant. "I mean your friend there is dead. He was your friend, wasn't he?"

"Look, this is ridiculous. Bob Welch personally asked me to ask around about Julie Glantz. He can't say he didn't."

"So you don't have anything else you want to tell us, professor? Just informally. Between you and us."

"I've told you everything."

"Okay. Well, we're going to need to take a formal statement from you, professor. You *will* be around this weekend?"

"Yes. But I swear I'm telling you exactly the truth. I can't understand why Welch would deny this. It's crazy."

"Okey-dokey. Well, you go home and sleep it on, professor, that's my advice. Watch yourself down these ladders, okay? We don't need two corpses in one night."

✢ 9.

Anika shivered against the bitter breeze, or from the fear and exhaustion that they both felt. He slipped off his jacket and put it around her shoulders. He felt a bit foolish once again performing such a clichéd chivalrous gesture, but she seemed to take it as a matter of course. Still he could not help a self-deprecating, mirthless laugh. "Sorry. You must think I'm trying to be one of knights of the roundtable. But, you looked cold."

She looked at him with a trace of puzzlement. "Why is it American men are always so bloody awkward about acting like men." He realized she was actually quite angry.

"Look, I'm sorry. I'm sorry about all of this awful evening."

"Don't apologize."

"I'm sorry—" he started again. They were passing by one of the fraternity houses where a Halloween party was obviously still in full swing. As they approached, the music suddenly stopped and the lights on the second floor went out. Gilpin was suddenly furious, furious at himself for the awkward idiot he was, furious at the idiocy and awfulness of Eric Travis's death, furious at his inability ever to do any damned thing right. He stopped and turned toward the second floor window of the fraternity house. "Don't you even *consider* throwing that water balloon," he shouted, pure distilled rage. The music immediately started up again and the lights came back on. They went on a few more paces before Anika broke out laughing in spite of herself.

"Look, I'm sor—" he tried once more. "Look, if you feel anything like the way I do you we both must be awful. Would you like to come back and have a drink? And then I can drive you home. My house is just two blocks that way."

"Okay."

They walked on a bit more in silence. "What did the police say?" she finally asked.

"They think it was a bizarre accident, maybe someone locked him in there as a practical joke and it went wrong. God, it was awful. His face—the look of torment. The medical examiner asked if he had a heart condition—apparently the shock was too much."

"I can't stop thinking that there we were, sitting there, listening to this music, while—while it was happening." She shuddered.

"Yeah, I know. Me too." They walked the rest of the short way to his house pensive and silent, their syncopated footsteps beating a lonely tattoo into the night. He unlocked the back door and held it open for her, following her up the short flight of stairs into his kitchen, whose functional, slightly severe lines were softened by a satin reflection of light coming from off the butcher block counters and the geometric leaded-glass doors of a large built-in cabinet that filled most of one wall.

"You have a lovely home," she said, filling with formal politeness the awkwardness of their suddenly being alone, facing one another in a small room, the cover of the dark and open night gone.

"Thank you. I did most of the work on the kitchen myself. The counters. And that cabinet. It was tricky fitting this against the place where the ceiling was curved, you see, and I had to scribe a line using dividers and then cut it with a jig saw and then keep cutting and refitting. And actually getting these hinges centered..." He realized he was babbling, explaining too much.

"I did not know that great literary theorists had so much mechanical sense," she said, a bit of her natural sarcasm returning, displacing the uncharacteristic awkwardness that had come over her a moment before.

"Well. I like working with wood. That's all. Sometimes I feel as if it's the only real thing I ever do—building a piece of furniture. You can actually touch it. Or kick it more like. But at least it's solid. So what would you like?" he asked, opening the cabinet and fussing around with glasses and bottles, feeling like an actor overplaying a bit part with too much stage business. "Not that there's much choice. I've got some single-malt Scotch. That Eric gave me. Dammit."

"Yes, I think that's what we had better have. Don't you? No ice—what do you call that—neat. What is this architectural style?" she said, hastily running her words together and pointing to the cabinet, urgently filling a vacuum that was threatening to implode with emotion.

"Oh—Arts and Crafts. Prairie."

"It's very American. Not fussy. Practical, but not severe. It's very nice."

"Well, thanks. Here you are," he said handing her her drink. "Why don't we go sit in the living room."

She took the only chair, he sat at the end of the sofa next to her. They both drank for a minute in silence.

"Would you like to hear some music?" he said, jumping up abruptly.

"Yes, maybe something, I don't know, gentle."

He flipped through some CDs on the shelf. "Brahms? Mozart—*Sonata Notturna?* Satie? Chopin? Schubert songs? No I guess not." He was babbling again. "Jazz—Connee Boswell?"

"Who is Connee Boswell?"

"Oh, wonderful singer from the '20s and '30s. Irving Berlin said she was the best ballad singer of the time, and Ella Fitzgerald said she learned how to sing a song listening to her. She's got this beautiful soft Louisiana accent." She nodded. He sat back down and the soft strains of Connee Boswell's supple voice drifted over them, mercifully filling the emptiness of the space between them.

Starlight, shining from the skies
Starlight, shining in your eyes
Oh sweetheart, what a night for you and me.

Under a blanket of blue
Just you and I beneath the stars.
Wrapped in the arms of sweet romance
The night is ours.

"There's something of a nightmare about all of this," he began quietly, his eyes turned downward, staring intently at his glass. "Surreal. It's as if somebody's playing a bizarre and very sick joke. Have you ever read any of classic English or American detective novels?"

She shook her head.

"Well, I know this sounds completely insane, but I swear everything that's happened in the last two days has come straight out of a famous detective story. There's a novel by Dorothy Sayers, *The Nine Tailors,* in which one of the characters dies when he is trapped inside the bell chamber of a church tower—dies from the deafening sound of the bells being rung. It's exactly the same thing. It's more than creepy. It's—well, sinister.

"And then both Julie and Eric got threatening notes that came right from another Sayers novel—*Gaudy Night*. It was in Latin, from Virgil, a passage about harpies. In *Gaudy Night* there's this woman, a college servant, whose husband had committed suicide after it turned out he had faked some research—destroyed a manuscript that contradicted his thesis.

"And so she was getting her revenge on the scholar who had exposed him, who was a woman; and in fact this woman, the servant, had a sort of crazed vendetta against all women scholars. She sent threatening anonymous notes, and one of them was exactly this same passage, word for word—I'm sure of it now. Monsters who have the body of a woman but are ravenous beasts that snatch the meat from men's mouths. No one suspected her because they figured a college servant wouldn't know Latin.

"But her husband had left that passage in his suicide note, you see. And Julie was sent this same identical passage. And Travis actually had a copy in his hand of it when he died. And on top of his copy it said something like 'I know what you're up to and you really can't.'

"And then there's this other whole business straight from *The Maltese Falcon* that's been happening." He described as best he could the events of the fat man and the missing manuscript, Julie Glantz's disappearance and the note she had left about visiting the organ chamber, his trashed office and the threatening emails. It sounded even more ridiculous and confused than ever, he knew, but he was in no shape to try to organize his thoughts; he was just grateful to have someone to pour it all out to.

"The whole idea in *The Maltese Falcon* is that there's this statue everyone is after," he continued. "It's supposed to be extremely valuable, but in the end it turns out that they've all been chasing a fake, totally worthless. The search for the statue does provide the motive for the murders and the mystery that unfold but it's really what Alfred Hitchcock called a McGuffin—it's a narrative contrivance that's designed to distract the audience.

"A kind of literary wild goose chase. The truth of disclosure as opposed to the truth of adequation: more about the structure of the narrative than the questions of actual guilt or innocence of the actors in the real sense. All mystery novels depend upon distraction to some extent, of course, to keep the reader guessing, but in the classic Agatha Christie type of mystery the story unfolds around the discovery of the truth. At least on the surface, it *is* about the truth of adequation, the logical piecing together of clues. It's the detective's narrowing down of possibilities that creates the underpinning of the narrative.

"But a McGuffin is actually a total cheat—the McGuffin is something all the characters are chasing after but in the end wasn't the real point at all. It's just a device to propel the plot—and confuse the audience."

She looked at him with an expression of exasperation. "But, Ted"—he realized this was the first time she had called him by his name, and felt a tingle on his neck—"you are talking bullshit again. This is real life, not some book. If someone is doing these things, none of this literary theory bullshit matters. They are either doing it or not. And they have a reason to do it. They are not concerned about a literary structure. Or a narrative. Or a plot."

"But it can't just be a coincidence."

"But life is not a text. A text has an author. What happens in a book is at the whim of the author's imagination. And unless someone is delusional, they do not act out in life the text of a book."

He stared at his drink. "I think the police think *I* have something to do with it. And God, I can see their point. I wrote a paper all about Dorothy Sayers and one about Dashiell Hammett for chrissake. I've been asking around about Julie, and I visited the organ chamber earlier in the day. And I think that policeman even thinks I trashed my own office and made up this business about the harpy message and sent that message to Eric myself. And it *was* completely idiotic of me to take it out of his hand like that."

She looked at him quickly, surprised.

"I didn't tell you that. It was in his hand. The message. I pulled it out of his hand. God knows why. Then the medical examiner said it looked like the message had been torn out of his hand in a struggle. Christ. It's funny you mentioned that word delusional—that was one of the key points in my paper. All search for explanation, all theory contains an element of delusion—that's what Freud thought. And that's what connects the world of the fictional detective and the real detective, you see. But if I were simply paranoid I'd think someone was setting me up. I mean every one of these 'clues' I've followed has put me in a suspicious position. So is that delusion or not?"

"Ted. I think you are tired and I think you are upset and I think you are talking bullshit."

He gave her a faint smile.

"I do not read detective novels but I know they rely on coincidences always meaning something," she went on. "The detective always just happens to be somewhere at exactly the right time, and, aha, he finds the clue. And not only does he find it, but he sees right away that it can only mean one thing. Case solved. Real life is never like that. Real life is full of coincidences that mean absolutely nothing. That is a law of statistics. There are far more patternless ways things can combine than patterned ways. You are so full of these ideas of finding meaning in structure you forget this. Why do any of these things have to be connected, to form a pattern, at all? It seems to me you have to take each of the facts one at a time, at least to start. Maybe some friend of Eric's did think locking him in there would be funny and didn't realize what would happen. Maybe these other things were someone playing a joke on *you*. Maybe this Julie is crazy and sending threats."

"Well, that's what Wendy Heatherton thought. She said the threatening note she got sounded like it had come from Julie. And—well, Julie certainly had a grudge against Wendy. And Eric, too—oh, geez. But I can't imagine she would do anything violent. Though there's no doubt she's been acting really strange. Damn, I just wish I knew for starters if this 'Great Jewish Foxhunters' business is real or not. Maybe this fat man just made up the whole thing. But I can't see why."

"Well, was this fat man looking for your McMuffin or for Julie herself, do you think?"

"McGuffin."

"Whatever."

"But that's a thought."

She thought for a minute. "This note that Eric had. Why do you think someone sent it to him?"

"Well. Julie had gotten the same thing. And I got one, not with the Virgil, but with a message saying something similar—'Your turn's coming.'"

"But 'Your turn's coming' is not the same as 'You can't do this.' And that is not a threat, exactly. Couldn't this be a copy of a message Eric had sent *to* someone? Maybe he was going to meet this person. Maybe he knew who was making these threats and was trying to stop him. Or her.'"

He stared at her. "My God, I think you're right. The Virgil was pasted in like it had come from another message. And the "you can't do this" wasn't in all capital letters like all of the others had been." He shook his head like a dog trying to get a fly off its nose. "You're right, you know, in mystery novels the detective always manages to make sense out of all the crazy disjointed clues. It's funny. Lord Peter Wimsey in the Dorothy Sayers novels is this sort of Renaissance man—he's an intellectual but also a man of the world, and he collects rare books and does delicate diplomatic missions for the British government and can play the piano and punch someone in the nose if he has to or gallop a horse down a beach and he also knows exactly what to say to be in command of any situation and draw out all kinds of different people. He acts like an upper class twit but actually is shrewd and charming and adept. And he has this perfect servant Bunter who looks after his every need and he never loses his cool."

He snorted. "I must be the anti-Lord Peter Wimsey. I'm always sticking my foot in my mouth. And getting upset. And not making sense of anything."

He looked around at the trails of dust on the living room floor. "*And* I've got this incredibly useless cleaning lady who breaks things."

He looked at the clock and then over to Anika and saw she was struggling to keep her eyes open. "Geez, I'm sorry. Oh God, I forgot I wasn't supposed to say that either. But here I've been talking and talking and you look exhausted. Maybe you'd like to stay. I've got a spare bedroom," he hastily added. "Oh, except my incredibly useless cleaning lady didn't make up that room this week. Let me find some sheets and a blanket." He got up and staggered a bit; the combination of two nights of little sleep, the evening's ordeal, and the Scotch came together like an unbalanced weight tipping him to one side.

"I think I will. Thank you," she replied, getting to her feet suddenly too. "Don't worry about the bed—you look very tired, also. Just tell me where the things are and I'll take care of it. Really."

He quickly went around turning out the lights and then led the way upstairs, showing her the spare room and bathroom.

While she was in the bathroom he went into his room and sat down on the bed. A wave of pure fatigue swept over him. He was trying to hold a thought in his spinning mind, to be sure to tell Anika where the spare blankets and pillows were.

But within a minute he was leaning back, sleeping the sleep of the dead.

✢ 10.

He dreamed he was being pursued in slow motion through a thick forest, the trees each turning into huge organ pipes as a shadowy form fell upon them in turn. Anika—a radiantly naked Anika, lithe and graceful, her blonde hair just grazing her bare shoulders—walked unperturbed from tree to tree in the distance ahead, her white body flashing out suddenly from behind the dark shapes, then just as suddenly disappearing.

He struggled to hold onto the dream, dark and frustrating as it was. But the sunlight glinting in through the window won out, and the vanishing dream finally eluded his last yearning grasp.

Along with the sun, his slowly awakening senses perceived something else, something softly brushing against his cheek. He opened his eyes into a mane of blonde hair.

Anika was lying next to him, a blanket pulled over the two of them. She was still wearing her clothes from the night before, but Gilpin could scarcely have been more astonished had she been naked. More astonishing still was the fact that he realized his arms were entwined around her shoulders and her waist, his face lying close to hers. He didn't dare move, not wanting to wake her, but at that moment her eyes flicked open. She raised an eyebrow and smiled.

"Hello," she said.

"Hello."

"I couldn't find the sheets and blankets last night, and you were completely out. Asleep. So..."

He hastened to extricate his arms. "Sorry. I guess while I was asleep I must have—well I must have imagined you were my old girlfriend or something and, just sort of automatically put my arms around you. I hope you don't..."

"That's very flattering."

"I mean, well, *she* was an incredible bitch, really."

"Even more flattering."

"Oh, God, why do I keep saying the wrong things. I mean, oh," but then he saw Anika was beginning to laugh at his distress, so he smiled sheepishly and stopped. "I mean," he began more deliberately, "I was having the most wonderful dream about you— and here you are."

"That is much better. That is very sweet."

His face fell.

"What's wrong?" she asked.

"Well, this old girlfriend..."

"The bitch."

"The bitch. She told me once that when a woman says a guy is 'sweet' it's the kiss of death. Almost as bad as 'nice.' It means she thinks he's harmless and boring."

She surveyed him with grave scrutiny. "Let me see. Boring? Mmmmm, no I don't think so. Harmless? Well, you don't act like a serial killer, which was why I thought it was probably safe for me to lie down here with you. And your house *is* freezing cold, you know."

"But look—you don't think I'm one of these morbidly sensitive guys who uses five different kinds of skin care products, do you? Because I'm not. I don't. Really. You could check my bathroom."

She gave another one of her short laughs, and leaned over and gave him a brief but very deliberate kiss on the lips, then sat up and swung her legs off the bed. "And now, I must go home and feed my poor cat." A small shadow crossed her face and she stood. "You know, for a few minutes I had completely forgotten about what happened last night. Here we were joking, and it wasn't until I thought of my poor cat just now that I thought of poor Eric. Poor Eric."

"Yes," Ted said weakly, "Poor Eric." He quickly got up, too. "Look, would you like some coffee or something. Oh. No that won't work, since my cleaning lady broke my coffee machine. Well, let me at least give you a ride home."

"No, that is all right. I still have my car at my work. And I'm going to come back and do some work after I go home to take care of Pi. I really need to get going. Now."

While she was getting ready he went downstairs, sat down at the piano, and softly played a rather ascetic Frescobaldi toccata, slow, measured, monkish. The contradictory impressions working on his feelings from her playfully encouraging teasing, her cool and almost indifferent self-possession, and his vivid dream of her left him feeling almost paralyzed in knowing what manner to take toward her.

But it was the dream that was still most vivid in his mind a few minutes later as he appeared at the bottom of the stairs, her handbag slung over her shoulder, her hair newly brushed and pulled into a soft pony tail. He jumped up and fumbled with the lock on the kitchen door to let her out. "Look, as long as you're coming back in, can't I well, take you to lunch?" he blurted out. "I really need to talk to someone more about all this. It would be—it would mean a lot to me. If you have the time."

"Ahh, so you are only interested in me for my brain. I should have known."

"Anika, I—"

"No, don't try. You'll just start apologizing again, and then I will have to get mad at you again. Yes, I will have lunch with you."

"Okay. Great. Thank you," he said with real feeling. "The Blue Olive? Twelve thirty?"

"Yes, fine."

He wondered whether he should kiss her, again—perfectly natural, saying goodbye—but the moment passed and she was

gone, and then he felt it had after all been right not to risk drain-
ing of meaning, through commonplace repetition, the singular
feeling her kissing him in bed had left within him.

He took a shower and got dressed and then tried calling
Welch's office, getting his voice mail. He left a message asking
him urgently to call. He managed to find an only-slightly expired
yogurt in the back of his refrigerator and ate it in his study as he
turned on his computer to check his email. Again there was a
message in his inbox that had appeared to come from himself:

Hegemonic Usurpation of Feminist Scholarship by "Men": Or, The Things Professor Ted Gilpin Will Do to Try to Get Laid

The problem of masculine identity is exacerbated to the
point of hypervisibility in the relation between the cultural
inscription of sexuality as gender and the erasure of sex in
the dominant construction of identity. By adopting the rhe-
torical "cover" of feminism, "sensitivity," and "equality,"
men are feverishly clutching at their/our genders and are
threatened by the knowledge that the sexually hegemonic
invisibility so long cultivated may now spell disappearance.
"Equalizing" gender categories
in the realm of scholarship will only succeed in suspend-
ing the history of sexism and making maleness, as opposed
to male privilege, visible.

In other words: Bugger off, bastard.

By the way, notice how all the trouble started after your
hot blond girlfriend showed up?

The style was definitely Julie's—that phrasing about "sexually
hegemonic invisibility" was unmistakably hers. But then the "by

the way" line at the end was just like the threatening taunt Julie herself had received.

The phone rang and he jumped for it. "Hello? Ted Gilpin speaking."

"Oh—Theodore. It's your mother."

"Yes, mom. Believe it or not, I haven't forgotten what your voice sounds like from the last time you called."

"Theodore, I'm sitting here and thinking and I had a question. I need to figure out what size turkey I should get for Thanksgiving. And I thought, maybe your new girlfriend is a vegetarian, so I won't need such a big turkey. So I thought I would call and ask. That's all."

"Mom—Thanksgiving is two months from now. I never said I was coming for Thanksgiving. I don't have a girlfriend. This woman is not my girlfriend. She's just a colleague of mine. Another professor."

"Well, I don't mean to pry, but I'm just wondering if maybe she's Jewish."

"No, mom. She's Dutch. From Holland. She's not Jewish."

"So, they don't have Jews in Holland?"

"Mom. Trust me, she's not Jewish."

"Well, as long as she's a nice girl. You know, your cousin Marv met this nice girl, and he took her last month to this special weekend for mixed couples they had at Grossinger's. They had a rabbi come and explain all about conversion. So, just something to think about."

"Mom. Please, don't keep talking like this. Now, I promise I'll let you know about Thanksgiving in plenty of time. Just not now. Say, mom. Did you—did you call the campus police the other day and tell them you were worried my office was going to be robbed?"

"Me? Why should I do a thing like that. I don't interfere in my son's life."

"So you didn't? Call them I mean?"

"No, of course not."

"You're sure?"

"Look, I may be sixty-seven years old, but I'm not completely meshugge yet. You think I could call the police and then forget I did it?"

"Okay, never mind. Thanks, mom. Look I've got to run. See you. Bye."

He was at the Blue Olive ridiculously early. North Ohio being perpetually seven years behind the rest of the country, the restaurant was decorated with bamboo blinds, hanging plants, and exposed brick walls painted in Crayola-crayon primary colors.

The Saturday crowd was sparse compared to the weekday crush, and he had no trouble getting a table. A young waitress tried twice to recite the specials but he said he was waiting for someone and he'd just wait to hear about them when she arrived.

Four patron-of-the-arts types at the next table wearing expensively casual-looking sweaters and chinos each had large martinis with olives sitting in front of them and were talking loudly about a combination piano recital and wine tasting they had attended the evening before: apparently this brilliant young music professor had a theory that the French vintages of the grands crus Bordeaux of the 1910s had directly influenced the music of Satie and Saint-Saens, and had obtained an NEH grant to buy cases of Chateau Lafite-Rothschild, Latour, and Margaux at thousands of dollars a bottle to demonstrate her idea.

Anika arrived twenty minutes late. He realized she had been wearing almost the same thing the two times he had seen her before, a white top and jeans, but now she was wearing black, again just a simple T-shirt, but the color was a stunning offset to her blonde hair and blue eyes. He gaped idiotically at her for a few seconds. She laughed. "God, Anika, you look—"

"No. We're here to be cerebral, remember?"

The waitress, impatient to have her cue at last, appeared at that instant and peremptorily interrupted with a "Let me tell you about our specials?" and began to recite an interminable list of ingredients, preparation methods, and presentations that left Ted with the vague feeling that when she was done he was going to be led into the kitchen to prepare his own entrée. "And last we have a pan-seared grouper, served on a bed of watercress and mango risotto. It's finished with a raspberry vinaigrette reduction and just a hint of fresh coriander."

His eyes wandered to the huge martinis at the next table. He was not much of a drinker usually. "I think I'm going to have a martini," he said with sudden conviction and a small laugh. "Not that I normally do, but—"

"Yes, good idea," Anika quickly agreed. "I don't either, but extenuating circumstances. Me, too. And I'll have the grouper." Ted ordered a crabcake that sounded from the waitress's description like it could have doubled as a small installation in an art gallery sculpture garden.

"I was thinking about what you said last night," he said when the waitress had gone. "About just taking facts one at a time and not trying to look too hard for patterns or form a theory right away. But that's not what *you* do. In science, I mean. You form a hypothesis, and you test it."

"Oh, congratulations, so you did a science-fair project in high school," Anika replied with deadpan scorn.

"Well, that's the scientific method. Everyone knows that."

"It may be, but it's not what scientists do. Most of what we do in science is explore where theory points you but is insufficient to take you yet. By definition that is the unknown. That is what is interesting. I mean, in molecular biology, astrophysics, medicine, you are always looking at complex things that you cannot possibly form an intelligent theory about ahead of time. And it would be a ridiculous waste of time to try."

"But the whole point is not just to gather disjointed facts—it's to explain it."

"Yes, but, you are looking at things backwards. Yes, the results of experiment are the raw material upon which ultimate explanations rest. But theory also guides and informs experiment. You don't waste your time spinning fanciful theories, as I just said. But you also don't waste your time pursuing experiments that are either trivial on the one hand or nonsensical on the other. And when you seek to develop a theory to explain something, you are drawing not just on data but also on the laws of physics, on all the established theory that has come before. It is like what I was telling you the other day, about how if you formulate a description, mathematically, of the mechanism correctly, you achieve new insights. Then *those* are the insights that point you where to explore further."

"But doesn't that constrain you to think in conventional ways? Or ways that are constrained by cultural bias? I mean, in like, well, yes the Sherlock Holmes stories, the police detective is always burying his nose in just the facts and Holmes uses his imagination to put things together in a way no one else sees. This was what I was saying about the almost delusional aspects of theorizing. You *have* to do that to achieve a new viewpoint, don't you?—I mean not be afraid of breaking boundaries. It's what Holmes says—once you eliminate the impossible, whatever remains, *however* improbable, must be the truth."

"Oh, yes, that is the line quoted by every crank and 9/11 conspiracy theorist and anti-science religious fanatic. No, what scientists do is not waste any time worrying about the impossible in the first place, because there is an infinite number of impossibilities. If you had to spend time eliminating the impossible you would never be done. If you aren't bound by reality or the laws of mathematics or physics or logic to begin with, then you can come up with a theory to connect anything to anything. Sparing yourself time-wasting absurdity is not a constraint."

"I still don't see it."

"Okay, I will give you an illustration." She took a paper napkin and pulled a pen from her pants pocket, and drew two axes of a graph. "On the x-axis I plot the number of letters a professor of literature has in his last name. On the y-axis I plot the number of times he has been laid in his life." She pronounced "laid" with an exaggerated American accent.

Her demonstration was interrupted by the simultaneous arrival of their drinks and food. "Sorry, we had a back-up at the bar," the waitress announced. "How is everything?"

Ted opened his mouth and was about to point out they hadn't had anything yet but caught himself. "Fine," he said. "Great. Everything's fine. Thanks."

Anika bit her lip to stop from smiling until the waitress left. "Okay," she continued. "So I put a point at six on the x-axis and one on the y-axis for the professor of literature who has six letters in his name and has been laid once in his life. Then I plot some other professors on this graph. And look, I can draw a curve through those points. Does that mean anything?"

He felt his ears burning red once again, and wished they wouldn't do that.

"And," she went on, "even if it did mean anything to draw a curve through them at all, it is a mathematical fact that I could draw an infinite number of different curves that pass through these same exact points. But unless there is some underlying mechanism that drives an actual relationship between these two variables, then all of these curves I draw are just bullshit. There is an infinite number of 'theories' I can invent that cover all the data points and still be wrong. The only basis I have for drawing any real curve is if I actually understand how one of the variables affects the other, and why."

Ted hesitated, about to attempt a nervous joke about her graph, but realized he couldn't outdo her deadpan humor, and thought better of it.

"And, this thing about cultural bias in science," she continued. "That is a license to go completely off the end and end up with no ground to stand upon at all. That is not theorizing—that is rendering the very meaning of theory nonsensical. And it is perpetrated by people who fall into exactly this error I am describing—they don't even understand what mathematics or physics is. You know the Sokal hoax, yes?"

"Well, a lot of people on the other side thought it was rather unfair. That he violated the trust of the editors."

"Unfair? He wrote a paper that was utter bullshit, and the humanists fell for it."

"But he did try to pass it off as a real paper."

"So why did they fall for it? Because he used all the right words about transgressing and privileging and hegemony and bullshit bullshit bullshit and at one point he even said that pi was formerly thought to be constant but now that it is seen in its 'ineluctable historicity,' the 'putative observer is fatally de-centered.' He said things like this all through the paper. But the real reason they fell for it was because there really are humanists writing about science like this, and they were so happy that here was a real physicist seeming to adopt their bullshit. I know because some feminist English professor sent me a paper once she had written about how 'masculine physics' had 'privileged' solid mechanics over fluid mechanics—this was because men have rigid sex organs and women have vaginal fluids. Of course, given how interested I thought men were in women's sex organs, I don't see why it shouldn't be the other way around. But this woman said this was why 'masculine' physics hadn't ever solved turbulent fluid flow. I wrote her back that once she had learned something about the mathematics of differential equations, she might understand why the Navier-Stokes equation is hard to solve, and then we could have an intelligent conversation on the topic."

"But look," he tried once more, "what about that crazy mathematician at Yale who just died, what's his name."

"Serge Lang."

"Right, Serge Lang. He was a brilliant mathematician, at least that's what the obituary in the *New York Times* said, but he went completely gaga, sending out these files of papers to hundreds of people trying to prove that AIDS isn't caused by a virus."

"So whoever said scientists aren't human? They make mistakes, too."

"But the whole point is that he was convinced that he was right, and all the more so because he believed he *was* following scientific reasoning. And actually I said he went gaga, but he wasn't—he was perfectly sane, it sounded like, a great scientist who had done hugely important work, but just arrogantly wrong about this thing. I mean, come on, Anika, this happens all the time—scientists confusing what is fundamentally a subjective prejudice or unsubstantiated belief with the objectivity and objective process of science. They start thinking that because they are scientists, then because *they* think something, it must be the product of science. And what does that say about whether there really is such a thing as objectivity in science?"

Ted realized with a start that she was looking at him with an expression of slightly surprised admiration, as if she was entertaining for the first time the remote possibility that he actually did have a brain. But she said nothing. He pulled one of the olives out of his drink and chewed it meditatively. "So what on earth should I do, Anika?"

"Ted, why ask me? I am no expert on crime. But it seems to me most crimes are not solved by Sherlock Holmes coming up with the brilliant theory that connects all the dots, but because of one or two perfectly ordinary leads the police follow, then somebody rats on the person or the person himself confesses. Isn't that the case? So don't do anything. Leave it to the police. They will find the person, who will probably turn out to be somebody who is a little crazy, and that will be the end of it."

"But, look, to be honest with you I'm starting to worry about what I told you last night. I don't think I was just being paranoid." He told her about the call to the police about his office. "Somebody is doing these things to try to get me involved in something.

And I got another one of those threatening emails just this morn-ing. And it's no joke now. It even mentioned you."

"And what did it say about me?"

"Oh, well, nothing really. It was, well..."

"Okay never mind." She looked at him with concern for a minute. "Okay, so if you have to do something, here's what I think. Just make an organized list of what you know for sure. And if it will make you feel better, I will read it and tell you what I think. But forget about theories. Really. Trust me on this, Ted. You have no head for it. I know that already."

"I'd like that. Thank you." The martini having worked its magic, too, by now, he felt remarkably better already. "You know it's funny, what I was saying last night about being the anti-Lord Peter. That paper I wrote about Dorothy Sayers was all about how the detective novel is an inherently patriarchal form and can't be regendered as a nonsexist narrative. But here we are and I'm play-ing the role of Harriet Vane and you're Lord Peter Wimsey."

"Who is Harriet Vane?"

Realizing the full implications of the analogy, he was suddenly embarrassed. "Oh, well she's the other, uh, protagonist in the sto-ries—she writes detective stories herself, you see, and is always stumbling into these crimes and trying to solve them but really in the end it's always Peter who, well saves the day." He decided not to mention the romantic attachment of Sayers's two characters. Somewhat impetuously he said instead, "Anika. How about if I made you a piece of furniture. For your place. I'd like to do that."

"Well, my apartment I'm afraid is not much. The usual physi-cist's rat hole. I still have all the boxes from when I moved here in the summer sitting around. I am not sure it deserves a Prairie Arts and Crafts hand-crafted by a famous literary theorist."

"Well, how about a coffee table. Or a bookcase. Or a chair."

She looked at him with a puzzled smile. "You know what you are like, Ted? You are like a choir boy, or a seminary student, who discovers that he does not believe in any of the elaborate theology of the Catholic Church. But the less he believes the more he rigidly follows it all to the letter, trying to convince himself he still really does believe. You believe in very simple things, I think. You like music, and poems, and furniture, and making things with your hands and you pretend to be into all of this complex literary theory but you don't believe it, really."

"I think those are apples and oranges," he replied, a bit stiffly. He pulled the second olive out of his drink and ate it and poked a bit at his vertical crabcake, which somehow was balanced on its edge, defying gravity by being glued to the plate with some viscous red sauce. A spring of watercress balanced precariously on top. "Well, anyway—I would like to make you something. I could make you dinner, if nothing else. I like to cook, too. And I owe you *something* for last night, and all of this trouble."

"Well, I have to get back to my work. And the next few days I am very busy. I can't make any commitments. But maybe I can find a minute to read your list. Of *facts*."

✤ 11.

A cold drizzle set in in the afternoon, with none of the soul-purging qualities of a good downpour; the buoying effects of lunch with Anika and even the artificial stimulus of the martini began to wear off, and the slow rain played on Gilpin's nerves like the relentless drip of a leaky faucet. He sat in Java Java Java Java for three quarters of an hour, watching the soggy joggers in their track suits come in for their decaf skim Sweet-and-Low chai lattes.

It was mid-afternoon before he finally sat himself down at his computer and tried to begin writing up his notes of the case. After a few minutes he wandered over to the bookshelf, hunted for a few titles, and plopped himself down in the armchair by the window of his study with Dorothy Sayers's *Gaudy Night*, Dashiell Hammet's *The Maltese Falcon,* and Anthony Berkeley's *The Poisoned Chocolates Case.* He read until the last outlines of gray sky were lost to the rapidly falling darkness of a sodden North Ohio autumn weekend night.

He found himself running over in his mind the scene in *Gaudy Night* where Harriet Vane writes the beginnings of a sonnet, and then inadvertently leaves it amid the description of the case she and Lord Peter Wimsey are investigating. How long had it been since he ever wrote a poem? That was a laugh.

But he sat back at his computer and began typing a few words and counting feet and thinking of what Anika had said to him about what it was he actually believed in; and, before he knew it, he had been lost to the effort and another hour and a half had passed, and there on the screen in front of him was the octave of a Petrarchan sonnet—Professor Ted Gilpin's poetical defense of what he does for a living, he thought to himself with a laugh:

> *To reach that view I climbed the tower stair:*
> *Forest, not trees; field, not grass; beach, not sand—*
> *To see the whole, to grasp, to understand*
> *What lower men did not dare think was there.*
> *To count each blade, each grain; to strip twigs bare—*
> *I might as well have stayed earthen bound and*
> *Spared myself the climb, keeping with the band*
> *Of slugs, who do not know, and do not care.*

Well, it wasn't completely execrable. He liked the stress shifts in the second line, emphasizing *forest, field,* and *beach.* And also on *earthen* in the sixth line.

The bitch was always resolving the octave with a sestet that turns the images on themselves, illuminates the theme from a different angle, resolves the questions raised. Unsurprisingly, he found himself stumped. Well, as Paul Fussell said, writing a good Petrarchan sonnet is difficult; writing a superb one is all but impossible.

He forced himself back to the real task at hand. His mind wandered over the jumble of facts, then back to the lines of his sonnet, and after going around in chaotic circles a few times he realized he was doing what he'd promised Anika he wouldn't.

But there seemed no other way to organize so many disparate loose ends except at least try to come up with an explanation for them. Better just to plunge in.

Okay, hypothesis 1. Julie Glantz has gone off her rocker, animated by her grudge against Travis. She's sending threatening notes to people, herself included. The fat man is just a coincidence. Probably was some joke of Travis's. There is no missing manuscript of Great Jewish Foxhunters. The email that referred to it was another joke of Travis's. Or maybe Julie sent that to herself in her delusions. She hatched this awful idea of tormenting Travis by locking him in the organ chamber; she was planning to, or maybe actually did, check out the organ the week before. She probably didn't think it would kill him, but did want revenge for his taking the money from her course.

He read back over what he'd written and decided it was even worse than his poem. Okay, second hypothesis. Some person unknown has a grudge against Travis. He was determined to get him, maybe even kill him; he's sent threatening notes to everyone else in the department to lay a false scent. The threats, however, pushed Julie over the edge and she's run away somewhere. The same conclusions about the mysterious manuscript apply.

Gilpin felt that was even more ridiculous, but pushed on and began typing even faster. Number three. Wendy Heatherton, professionally jealous of Julie, tries to push her into cracking up by sending her threatening notes. Julie really is doing some outside project, and Wendy thinks if she finds out what it is she can also use that against her. Julie cracks up and vanishes. Wendy learns of Welch's request to Ted to look into the matter and starts leaning on him to reveal what he knows. Travis stumbles on the truth and plans to confront Wendy and sends her a note to meet him before the organ concert, but she struggles with him and he drops dead of a heart attack, and she locks him in the organ chamber. She is trying to kill two birds with one stone by making Gilpin look like he's involved in both matters.

Boy does that stink

Okay, four. The fat man really has commissioned a manuscript from Julie; he's obsessional and was threatening Julie unless she delivered it and Travis tried to stop him and...Oh, the hell with it.

Well, if only he could find the manuscript, if it existed, maybe that would clear up everything. Well, not everything, but something. Of course, in *The Maltese Falcon,* the statue ended up being nothing—the McGuffin indeed. A brief disturbing idea flitted into his mind; the email he had received that morning, its allusion to Anika; and then the beautiful but evil girl who's the antagonist in *The Maltese Falcon*—"I won't play the sap for you," Sam Spade tells her at the end, after he realizes she's been the cause of the whole trail of mayhem and violence and murder he's been dragged through, naively mistaking her beauty for goodness.

God, he was getting really paranoid, Gilpin thought. Anyway, she was a redhead. Better stop now. He printed out what he had done, threw it in a folder, ate a few left-overs, and went to an exhausted sleep.

On Sunday he tried calling Welch four more times, still no success, and left two more voice messages. At one o'clock the two policemen rang his doorbell unannounced and stayed until four, having him tell his story over and over again.

Late in the day he suddenly decided to go the gym, animated by a wistful hope he might run into Anika. But he had the place almost to himself, swam a dozen laps of the world's most unconvincing breast stroke in the deserted pool, then took himself home, dissatisfied, empty, his eyes smarting a bit from the chlorine.

As he passed Java Java Java Java on the way back, a young woman who had been typing furiously away at a computer at a table by the window looked up and waved through the glass. Ted broke his stride and entered the shop.

"God, Ted, you look like a lovesick moose," she said as he sat down at the table with her.

"Hi Mary."

"I said, you look like a lovesick moose."

"And what is a lovesick moose supposed to look like?"

"Got a mirror?"

"Okay." He sighed.

"As your attorney, I advise you to tell me all about it."

He let out a mirthless laugh. "Actually, I may be needing a

lawyer before long. But, oh damn, I guess you're right about the lovesick part."

She took off a pair of serious-looking octagonal-lens glasses, which had the immediate effect of making her babyishly round face look even younger. Gilpin suspected the lenses were plain glass, necessary defensive camouflage for the youngest female assistant professor in the law school, who had the fortune, or misfortune, of constantly being mistaken for a prospective freshman when she walked around the campus.

She ran a careless hand over the top of her short hair and closed her laptop.

"That's a relief," she said. "Because if it were a legal problem, I'd have to add you my ever-growing list of ingrate friends who always seem to look on me as a font of free legal advice. Which is pretty funny, since they're usually getting divorces or suing real estate agents and all I teach these days is this half-assed course on international anti-terrorism financing law so the dean can put on the law school website some horseshit about how we're 'globalizing the curriculum.' Which I finally figured out is a fancy way of saying that if we can get more sons of dictators to come, they might give us money for our endowment some day. But enough about me. Tell Auntie Mary, J.D., all about your heartbreaks."

"Okay Mary, let me just say it. Do you think a beautiful, brilliant woman who could have any guy in the universe she waved her little pinkie at would look twice at a putz like me?"

"Well, you know Ted, I can say from personal experience that women really just love it when guys go around sounding like Eeyore. You've almost got it down perfectly. You might work on it just a bit more and I'm sure she'll be so overcome she'll like rip her bra off next time she sees you."

"Yeah, okay. But look, I understand that women don't like nice guys. Nice is deadly. Nice is safe and boring. Okay, I can sort of get that. But for chrissake, what's the alternative? I mean I *am* a nice guy, I think. What am I supposed to do, start slapping her around or something? And here I am thirty-four years old, and I still can't figure out what the hell is going on when a woman seems to like me and we seem to connect but she doesn't really give me one iota of encouragement beyond that."

He briefly described what had happened Friday night.

"God, Ted, I'm sorry about Eric—I hadn't even heard about this." She asked the inevitable ghoulish curious questions, he mechanically answering, until her sympathy for his obvious discomfort at last outweighed her otherwise relentless instinct for cross-examination.

"But you know you are a nice guy," she said, returning to the previous subject. "That's why you're one of my best friends. But you're wrong about women not liking nice. For a lot of women nice is very good. It's just that there has to be something else, too. Nice and even shy and vulnerable is great, in fact, as long as there's some—I don't know, masterfulness to go along with it."

Ted looked glummer than ever.

"And since you are so in such desperate need of bucking up, I'll tell you something I've never said before—I almost thought I'd made a big mistake the first time I heard you play the piano, which for some reason wasn't for months and months after I met you and had been eating your meals and drinking your wine and pouring my heart out to you about my problems with fuckhead. That's when I realized you weren't just some nice, if geeky, intellectual. Though it was too late then. And I was completely tied up with fuckhead at that point anyway. I probably still would be, and still pouring my heart to you about it, if he hadn't got that offer from Harvard. A blessing to all concerned. Your department in particular, from what I hear."

They sat in silence for a minute while Ted took this in.

"So, did you play something for her?" she asked.

"Well, yes, I did play a tune while she was upstairs getting ready to leave on Saturday morning. I guess she heard me."

"What did you play?"

"Uh, a Renaissance keyboard piece. Uh, a toccata, actually."
He was losing his nerve under her scornful expression.
"Frescobaldi."

She screwed up her face. "Oh, God, Ted. *Not* Frescobaldi.
Tell me anything but Frescobaldi. Not one of those slow ones with
all the double whole notes?"

Ted looked away.

"They really shouldn't let you out in public. She's probably
convinced you're some excruciatingly sensitive aesthete who was
brought up in a commune by hippies or baboons or something.
Why couldn't you have played 'Ain't Misbehavin'? That's what
gave me a definite twinge, that time I heard you letting loose on
that. I suddenly realized you had far more going for you than met
the eye."

Ted sat looking morosely at the table top.

"Alright Ted. Here it is. Play some jazz on the piano. Cook
her a great dinner, and not some precious little thing from the
Silver Palate Cookbook like fuckhead used to make to try to im-
press me—you know he actually used to put doilies on the table
and would spit out the wine at wine tastings—but one of those Indian or Mexican dishes you do with tons of spices and throwing
the pans around and leaving the kitchen looking like a terrorist
just hit the place. And be your usual sweet good nice self, and
treat her like a perfect lady, and act like you are completely, morally, one hundred percent certain that, like the perfect lady she is,
she wants nothing more in the world than to leap on top of you
the first chance she gets. Okay? This is sound legal advice, but
please note I am not admitted in Ohio."

"Okay, thanks Mary. You're a gem."

"You're not so bad yourself. Now you want to tell me about
this legal problem you mentioned? Is this something to do with
this business about Eric Travis? That must have been awful Friday
night."

"Well, actually, the police warned me not to talk about it to anyone. I was really just kidding about needing a lawyer. I think. Anyway—I'm sure it was just a terrible accident and that'll be the end of it."

She looked quizzically at him. "Alright, well take care, Ted. This is just standard advice, but you should have a lawyer present if the police ask you for any further formal statement. Now, I've got to finish this thing"—she pointed at her computer—"I'm trying to engineer my escape from Welch's Internationalization Task Force Strategy Implementation Development Working Group Retreat. I told them last time that preservative fumes from the donuts they set out for the breaks trigger my migraines, but I think they're getting suspicious. So I'm trying to draft a legal opinion that it's actually a conflict of interest for me to be on this committee. It's taking me hours, but all in all a sound investment of my time."

She opened her laptop and put her glasses back on. "Alright buster, buzz off, smile, and never, ever, refer to a wine as 'buttery.' Do what I say and you'll have to get an electric cow prod to keep her away from you so you can get any work done."

✤ 12.

Monday morning's class was interminable.

But when Gilpin got back to his office there was an email message from Welch saying he had tried to phone and asking Gilpin to call him back. He quickly picked up the phone and dialed. It was answered on the second ring by Welch himself.

"Bob, hi. I'm glad I got hold of you."

"Ted, just wanted to tell you how we're very closely monitoring this situation here at the C-level. I want you all to know we are a hundred percent behind our folks at a tragic time like this. And we're arranging to have counselors available for anyone there in your department. We are *supporting* our people, Ted. That's what we do here."

"Uh, thanks Bob. Look, Bob, I'm a little concerned about one thing. That's why I kept trying to reach you. You see the police had asked me about why I was asking about Julie Glantz, and so I told them you had asked me to do this. And they seem to have this idea that you told them you didn't ask me to do this. So I'm wondering how they could have got that idea. Because you did. I mean ask me. Right?"

"Ted, I sympathize a hundred percent. I hear what you're saying."

"Bob. Did you tell them you *hadn't* asked me to look into where Julie was?"

"Ted, sounds like just a miscommunication issue. Ted, part of how I always approach solutioning a problem is to step up to the plate myself. It's the way I am, Ted. Not a matter of claiming credit—a matter of taking responsibility. *Loyalty*, Ted. I don't leave my team twisting in the wind. And I'm sure you appreciate that."

"So...you didn't actually tell them you had asked me to do this job for you."

"Ted, I want to assure you I took full responsibility on this one myself. It's what I like to call the broad shoulders policy. Now, let me and my team here know if there's anything you folks need, right? We're going to pull through this together. That's a commitment. So long, Ted. When this blows over, we'll have to have that round of golf we always keep talking about. Right?"

"Uh. Right."

"Attaboy, Ted. Hang in there."

The persistent drizzly weather added to the pall of Travis's death to make the usual gloom of the third floor more oppressive than Gilpin thought possible. In mid-afternoon Wendy Heatherton came in with a smirk on her face. "You noticed dog boy hasn't been in today?" she said, brandishing a piece of paper.

"Um. What's that, Wendy?"

She slapped it down on his desk. "It's a ruling from the Committee on Gender Sensitivity. A total vindication of the rights of People of Allergy and Chemical Sensitivity."

"Oh. So you mean no dogs anymore."

"No dogs is right." Her gloating was unbearably snarky. "I bet dog boy is so pissed off he's gone home to kill himself."

"Wendy, come on. That's a rather insensitive thing to say yourself. And especially after Eric and all."

She eyed him with contemptuous surprise. "So. Ted Gilpin's suddenly got some balls, himself. That hot blonde you're following around like a demented basset hound been stimulating your hormonal system?"

"What was that you called her?"

"Hot. Blonde. New vocabulary words for you?"

"Okay, never mind. I just don't think you should gloat about this. You won, so why rub it in?" She gave another smug smile and left.

It was at four, just before dusk that the first of the calls came. He answered and heard a click almost as soon as he started to speak. It happened again at four thirty and four forty five. At five twenty it was fully dark and the phone rang again. He picked it up with irritation. "Hello," he said wearily.

"Professor Gilpin?" an official-sounding voice said. The connection was crackly and had a metallic echo, like a bad cell-phone link.

"Yes?"

"This is officer..." the name was obscured in a barrage of static.

"I'm sorry, this is a bad connection. I can barely hear you."

"Professor, this is..." again the name was lost "...campus police. Can you come down to the lagoon. It's urgent."

"Um. Can you tell me what this is about? And who did you say you were?"

There has a loud crackle and a gonging sound and the connection cut off. "Damn," said Gilpin. He dialed the campus police.

"Lawless Police."

"This is Professor Gilpin. Did someone from your department just try to call me? It sounded like it was on a cell phone, and then was cut off."

"Just a minute, sir," the efficient and impersonal female voice responded. He waited several minutes.

"Lawless Police. Can I help you?" the voice came back on.

He repeated his request.

"Can you hold, please."

"Look, no—just."

He heard the click and the empty-space sound. He waited several more minutes. Finally the woman came back on once again. "Sir, if a cell phone call was placed to you, we would not know that."

"Look, it was someone who said he was an officer and needed

me to come to the lagoon. Do you have any information about that?"

"I am sorry, sir. We cannot give out any information about ongoing police activity."

"But—"

"Can you hold, sir?"

He hung up. He tapped his fingers on his desk a few times. Then he abruptly got up, put on his coat, and hurried down the hall and the stairs. Walking across the quadrangle he followed a few paces behind a student talking on her cell phone. Snatches of inane conversation drifted back to him. "No, I'm on my cell...I'm walking across the quad...I'm at the sculpture thing...no, I'm wearing my jeans...*you* know...duu-uuuhhh, the ones I got at Urban Outfitters? hel-*lo*..." He finally got past her and strode quickly across the street to the path to the lagoon.

There was no sign of a police car—or anything, or anyone, else for that matter. The streetlamps that lined the gravel path cast pools of light every twenty-five yards along the edge of the water. He had just reached the far end of the pond when he caught sight of some small form darting out of the edge of one of the circles of light ahead, into the darkness.

As he got closer he heard a whining sound. A small Scottie dog was running frantically back and forth between a leather briefcase leaned up against one of the benches, which was in the light, and the edge of the gravel beach by the water, which was in darkness. Gilpin turned off the path.

"Tyrone?" he called uncertainly. The dog froze, stared at him, then resumed his back and forth running. Then Gilpin froze. A figure lay slumped on the gravel. He ran forward.

"Mfuka? Are you okay?" His head was bent at an awkward angle. He reached out to touch it, then recoiled from the warm wetness. He looked at his hand and saw it was covered with bright red blood.

"Jesus Christ," he said. Shaking, he managed to get his cell phone out of his pocket and dialed the campus police emergency number.

"Lawless Police," said the same voice he had spoken with a few minutes before.

"Yes, this is Professor Gilpin. I'm here at the lagoon and..."

"I'm sorry, sir. As I told you, we are not permitted..."

"Look. Please listen to me. I came down here myself. After I spoke to you just now. There's somebody seriously injured here. It's an emergency. There's—a lot of blood. Please come quickly."

There was a pause and some clicking sounds. "Where did you say you were?"

"At the lagoon. The far side." His voice was shaking.

"Sir, I need you to remain calm."

"How the hell can I remain calm?" he shouted.

"Sir, I *need* you to remain calm."

"What is this, something they teach you in 911 school? For crissake, my colleague is here with blood all over him. And oh my God, it looks like his throat's slit. Jesus."

"Now, sir, if you'll just remain calm we'll have someone there right away."

"You're going to keep saying that, aren't you?" he yelled into the phone.

"Sir, if you'll..." Gilpin threw his phone furiously into the lagoon. He heard it ricochet off one of the dead-goose decoys with a hollow thud and splash into the water.

He sat down on the bench and tried to call the dog over to him. Tyrone finally came up to the bench, and then with a sudden spring jumped into his lap. He sat there mechanically petting the dog until the police arrived.

It was a different pair of cops this time; they had him sit in the passenger seat of their patrol car while they went through their routine, stringing yellow tape around the scene, talking incessantly on their radios, consulting with the cavalcade of EMTs, crime scene technicians, and men in old fashioned trench coats who appeared and stood by calmly taking in the proceedings. The door of the police cruiser opened and Gilpin looked over to see his friend the sergeant slide into the driver's seat. Tyrone, still sitting on his lap, growled suspiciously.

"Professor, you have a way of being on the scene, I'll give you credit for that," the sergeant said with elaborate nonchalance.

"Look. Somebody called me. They said they were a police officer. They asked me to come down here. And I found him."

"That's what the dispatcher told me, professor. Only nobody from our department called you. That's a fact."

"Well, Jesus Christ. I mean this is too much. Somebody keeps trying to drag me into these things."

"You seen this, before, professor?" He was holding an evidence bag containing a seven-inch long knife with a deeply hollow-ground blade and a wrapped leather handle. "It appears to be the weapon that was used." Gilpin reluctantly took the bag that the sergeant held out to him. It was still stained a dark crimson.

"I think I have. I think it's one of the things Professor Shalaby had in his office."

"Shalaby?"

"Yeah. He collected these kinds of things. American military ordnance. And stuff....Jesus Christ. Was it—did somebody kill him?"

"We can't answer that yet, professor. It's a bit unusual for someone to commit suicide by slitting their own throat, you know, but not impossible. That's for the ME to determine. That Professor Bariki's dog?" the sergeant said, eyeing the Scottie, who had continued his growling.

"Yes. Yes, it is. He was here. By the—body. Running around."

"Nice looking fellow. He didn't have a wife or girlfriend, I understand. Who's going to take care of the dog, you think?"

"Geez. I dunno. I suppose, well, I could keep him. For a while anyway. I don't know what else to do."

The cop kept looking at the dog and said matter of factly,

"Now, professor, this business of the phone call. You're sure you got this phone call at all? I mean, the stress and all—maybe you're a little mistaken. Maybe you're a little mistaken about some of the other things you told us, too. Perfectly understandable. Could happen to anybody. But we know definitely no one from our department called you. We've checked. Everything. So how's about you telling me everything from the beginning. One more time?"

"Oh, God, not again. Look. You've got to know one thing. There's something really bizarre happening here. I know you're going to think this is nuts, but both of these—deaths. They're right out of famous murder mysteries. By Dorothy Sayers. I wrote a paper on Sayers, that's how I happen to know. But I mean, you can look it up yourself. Travis—it's how the victim dies in *The Nine Tailors.* And this—this is exactly what happens in *Have His Carcase.* The victim is found with his throat cut. On a beach. Well, alright, this isn't exactly a beach. But you know."

The cop looked at him for a minute with a level gaze. "Professor, I'm sure you've had a very trying experience here. Now let's just taking it from the beginning, okey-dokey?"

He told his story over and over; to the sergeant, to a plainsclothes detective who took his place after half an hour and peered at Gilpin through half-closed eyes, to the sergeant again, to a woman cop who looked like she could have pulled his neck off with her bare hands, to the chief of the campus police who appeared on the scene wearing a uniform with stripes all the way up his sleeve. The woman cop came back and took his fingerprints— "just routine," she said fiercely—and then finally the two original cops drove him home.

He carried Tyrone up the back steps and placed him gently down on his kitchen floor. He filled a cereal bowl with water for the dog, and fed him some slices of ham from the refrigerator.

It was true what he had said to Anika about not being much of a drinker, but he got out the bottle of single malt Scotch, emptied the remaining contents into a twelve-ounce water glass, filling it nearly three-fourths full, and lay down on his sofa and emptied the glass in ten minutes of steady effort. The last thing he remembered before mercifully losing consciousness was the sound of the Scottie gently snoring from his spot curled up on the sofa next to him, his head resting proprietarily on Gilpin's chest.

✛ 13.

In spite of Mary's pep talk, Ted found himself glumly brooding that it must have been no more than sympathy or curiosity that prompted Anika to phone him late Tuesday morning, aghast at the news, and offering to come to dinner that night. But the intoxicating power of anticipation soon had conquered even the shock and gloom; and at one point in the afternoon he realized he had spent twenty minutes imagining what her calves looked like, until he angrily and guiltily roused himself from his obsessive reverie.

She came as promised at 6:30, wearing a red patterned print top and a softly feminine, flowery mid-length skirt that took his breath away when he opened the door. He started to say something to her, but the scene was interrupted at once by Tyrone who came streaking into the kitchen, barking furiously and scrambling to keep a grip on the varnished wooden floor as he turned the corner. For a few seconds it looked like he would make it, but then with a final skittering of dog toenails he capsized and slid the last six feet on his side into Anika's bare legs.

She dissolved in laughter, then gravely greeted the dog and tried to pet him; and by then any thought of giving her a kiss or saying anything right was gone.

"Ted, I am so sorry about this terrible business. I feel it is even wrong for me to be laughing now. I did not know you had a dog. He is new?"

"No. This is Mfuka's dog. I've just sort of ended up taking care of him for a while. He seems to like it here, though. Mfuka was always talking about all his behavioral problems, but he's doing fine, actually. A hell of a lot better than I am, to be honest with you. Well, come in. I'm very glad you came. I—I ended up canceling my classes today, and just staying here. But I—well, what kept me going was thinking of seeing you tonight. Really."

They sat in the living room again. He told her about what had happened on Monday night, sparing her the gorier details. "The one thing I didn't tell the police was the way it's all reminded me of some *other* detective stories. I mean, besides the Sayers ones. I guess I thought they were already thinking I was crazy enough as it was. So I didn't tell them at all about *The Maltese Falcon* business. But you know what happened to me last night was also right out of an Agathie Christie story, *The Murder of Roger Ackroyd.* He's killed with an ornamental knife. And the narrator gets a phone call summoning him to the scene of the crime. Only the butler who's supposed to have made the call swears he didn't."

"And why is he called then?"

"Uh, well. Actually. The murderer is the narrator himself. It's a famous story—because of that twist, you see. And he does really get the call. Only he's arranged it ahead of time. To cover up for himself. I guess that's part of why I didn't feel exactly like bringing it up," he added feebly.

"I see."

He handed her the folder with his notes. "So. Anyway. Here's what I've done. Maybe you'd like to read it while I finish getting dinner ready."

She opened it and started to read but stopped after a few seconds. Ted, still standing there, sheepishly avoided her gaze. "Ted, I cannot *believe* this," she said. "You have made theories anyway—after all we talked about on Saturday. I thought you agreed you would just organize the facts."

"Well, I started to, but then I just kept thinking about—well, there's this famous detective story. *The Poisoned Chocolates*

Case." She rolled her eyes. "Well, I was looking at it after I saw you Saturday. And trying to think about all of this. You see, the whole idea of this book is really that facts in and of themselves are insufficient. Everyone can interpret facts so many different ways. So you *have* to try to *solve* the case—if for no other reason than to see where you go wrong. It's only by building hypotheses, and even more important by breaking down the incorrect hypotheses of others, that you can arrive at the solution."

"Ted, why are you using a made-up story as your reference point?"

"But it's not just an ordinary detective story. It's a detective story about the very methodology of detective fiction. It's really a very modernistic analysis of meaning and structure, even though it was published in 1929."

He saw the look of contempt on her face deepening. "Look, just hear me out. The idea of the story is that there's this club of six armchair detectives. There's a brilliant novelist, and a dramatist, and two crime writers, and a famous defense lawyer. And they decide to reexamine a certain famous unsolved murder. Each week they get together and hear the solution that each member has come up with in turn. And of course the point is that each one comes up with a completely different solution, using more or less the same facts. It's only the very last member, who's sort of this apologetic sad-sack type, who uses where the others have gone wrong to actually come up with the correct solution."

"And so what is the case that they solve?" Anika asked, in spite of herself.

"Well it takes place in London. And this baronet, who's sort of a libertine, gets a box of chocolates delivered to him at his club. There's a note from the manufacturer saying it's a free sample of a new assortment of chocolates being sent to important people. The baronet is disgusted with this commercialism and is about to throw it away, but a fellow member of the club who happens to be sitting there when he opens the box says he needs a box of chocolates to settle a bet he's lost with his wife, so he offers to take them from him. So he takes the chocolates home, and he and his wife eat some of them. He becomes violently ill but recovers, but his wife, who's eaten more of them, dies. The police find that the manufacturer hasn't been producing any new assortment of chocolates or sending out any free sample boxes at all. Somebody apparently got hold of a piece of the company's notepaper to forge the note and mailed it to the baronet. And the chocolates were injected with nitrobenzene by someone who'd taken them out of their wrappers and then carefully rewrapped them.

"But all of the obvious leads go nowhere, and the police finally give up on the case, deciding that some unknown lunatic must have sent them and that's the end of it. And so, as I said, each one of the six members of the club devises a completely different solution. It's a bit contrived, and the author does cheat a bit by introducing new facts along the way that the reader couldn't possibly have known about, but it's still really brilliant. And if you read it, you'll see my point. You just *can't* get away from trying out inferences and testing solutions."

"Okay," Anika said with a sigh. "I will be scrupulously fair to the bullshit of the postmodern scholars of the humanities. Do you have this book here?"

Ted went upstairs and brought it back to her. "Here you are. Look, I'll go finish making dinner now like I said and you can just sit here and make yourself comfortable and read. Would you like a glass of wine or something?"

"Good idea," she said drily. "Better leave the bottle."

The rhythm of cooking, the feeling of his hands performing accustomed tasks that demanded mental concentration but exacted no great mental strain, soon took its familiar calming hold of him in the kitchen. He took from a bag in the cupboard ten of the large dried New Mexico chiles he had managed to eke out of his far-too-shady backyard garden plot this summer; in a heavy pan, no oil or water, he slowly toasted them over a low flame until the room was filled with their complex blend of heat and earth smells.

He broke off the stemmy tops with a satisfying crack, shook out the seeds, chopped them roughly, and returned them to the pan with some water. While they were simmering he quickly pressed out a dozen tortillas, quickly cooking them in a skillet. He always challenged himself to see how quickly he could get a dish like this assembled and in the oven: his one real streak of Type A competitive instinct.

It was exactly nineteen minutes by the kitchen clock when he banged the oven door shut behind the dish. He had the guacamole ready in ten more minutes and was just giving a final squeeze of lime to it when Anika peeked around the corner.

"It smells wonderful."

"Dinner is served, madame," he said in a terrible French accent, terrible even as a fake French accent.

"Mademoiselle," she corrected, her accent flawless. "And what are we having?"

"Oh, just something simple I whipped up—Mexican. Enchiladas colorados, guacamole, flan for dessert. But I did make it all myself, from scratch. And I grew the chile peppers in my garden."

"You know, for a guy who usually apologizes every two minutes, you seem very boastful when you get into a kitchen."

"Sorry. I mean, dammit. Well, okay, maybe it is my weak spot. Anyway—let's eat."

They ate for a few minutes. "Ted, okay, I've skimmed through your Mr. Berkeley's brilliant book while you are cooking this simple but, of course, perfect dinner."

"Thank you. And?"

"And you have got the complete wrong end of it. As always."

"What do you mean? How?"

"So, I am not a brilliant literary theorist, but it seemed perfectly obvious to me that all he is actually doing is making fun of the whole genre of detective stories."

"Well, yes and no. He is having some fun with it. But he's also making a very important statement about the nature of truth, and how it is constructed from differing point of view."

"Ted, come on. The whole point of the book is to show how phony detective stories are. He even has this guy Chitterwick at the end make that chart showing the approach each of the others have used. And these are, every one of them, all the clichéd methods of detectives in fiction, yes? I mean, even I know that and I don't read detective stories. There's one who asks cui bono; and another who looks for the woman; and another who studies the character of the individual. And each of the different methods of proof are also represented: deduction, induction, and a blend of deduction and induction, and scientific deduction, and intuition. And psychology. So he has each one of these solutions presented, and then each one is exposed as a fallacy. One of the members of the club, when it's his turn, he even proves that he is the murderer himself—which is obviously a joke, yes?"

"Yes, but at the end it's only by analyzing what's wrong with each of these other theories that Chitterwick gets the right answer."

"No, I disagree. The author's whole point is that by the normal rules of the detective story, every one of these other solutions is perfectly good. It's just that in the normal detective story nobody then comes along and exposes what a fraud has been committed on the reader. But in this book, Berkeley has all of his detectives each take the exact same clues and deduce six or seven different things from the same piece of evidence, one after another. There is a place where he says just that."

She flipped through the book. "Yes, here it is. This is right after Chitterwick shows his chart. He says, 'I have often noticed, that in books of that kind'—he means detective stories—'it is frequently assumed that any given fact can admit of only one single deduction, and that invariably the right one. Nobody else is capable of drawing any deductions at all but the author's favorite detective, and the ones he draws are invariably right.'

"And then the detective-story writer, Bradley, answers, 'I'll write a book for you, Mr. Chitterwick, in which the detective shall draw six contradictory deductions from each fact. He'll probably end up by arresting seventy-two different people for the murder and committing suicide because he finds afterwards that he must have done it himself. I'll dedicate the book to you.' And then Chitterwick says, "Yes, do. For really, it wouldn't be far from what we've had in this case. In fact, it was as much as anything the different deductions drawn by different members that proved their different cases.' So—the more they theorize, the wronger they all are.

"The point is, Ted, if you have already decided on the solution, you can always dream up some way of making the evidence fit. I noticed that when nothing else works, the detective just says, aha the murderer was so clever, he left this piece of evidence deliberately just to mislead us. You can explain anything with that trick."

"But, look, Anika, there's another place, I think a little farther on, where Chitterwick says that everybody got remarkably close to the truth, and that it was only because he was the last person to try, and had taken notes on all the failed efforts that preceded his, that he was able to arrive at the truth himself."

"Yes, but then *his* solution depends on exactly the same trick he himself criticizes. He just comes out with his clever solution and asserts that it's correct because it covers the facts and that it's the only possible deduction. I mean, maybe this was unintended irony.

"But Chitterwick goes through this whole point of showing how everyone, for example, deduces a different conclusion from just the business of the notepaper. One says the notepaper proves the murderer must have worked at the chocolate company. Another says, no, the murderer must have needed to use this particular brand of chocolates because the intended victim liked them, and so he then found a way to get the company's notepaper. Another says, no, he just happened to have access to a piece of the company's notepaper, and that's what gave him the idea of then using the chocolates in the first place.

"And then Chitterwick comes in at the end says that the notepaper was used only because it was intended to falsely implicate someone, who could be shown to have had access to the notepaper. But he—what's that expression—he pulls the rabbit out of the hat, too. It seems to me what Berkeley is saying is that in a normal detective story the author basically plays a trick by presenting only one solution, deliberately ignoring all the other possibilities. And the reason the author *has* to do this is because—just like his phony fictional detectives—he really has started from his solution and worked it out backwards."

"But, Anika, I think the only reason the other detectives get gummed up in this story is because the actual murderer turns out to be a writer of fiction herself. And she has constructed a plot that's designed to be deliberately misleading—it's meant to cast guilt on the wrong person."

"Ted. So you are saying the only reason that the theorizing by a group of fictional characters in a fictional detective story did not work out was because the murder had been committed by a fictional character who is a fictional author of fictional detective stories, and so she planned and committed a murder according to the conventions of detective fiction."

"Uh, something like that, yes."

"Whereas if they had been trying to solve a murder plot merely written by a real writer of fictional detective stories, it would have worked out fine."

"Oh." He felt an ache in his forehead.

"But, look," he tried once more, "the police in the story do exactly what you say I should be doing, just sticking to the facts. And they fail, too. See, Chitterwick puts them on the chart, too." He pointed to the bottom of that page. "They confine themselves to material clues, and take a general view, and use routine police methods. And all they come up with is that some unknown fanatic was the killer."

"But this is also a joke. This is also the cliché of all detective stories, isn't it? That the police are stupid and can't see beyond the obvious facts, and then the brilliant detective comes along and shows them up. And of course Mr. Berkeley is even making fun of that point because he has Chitterwick, this—what did you call him—sad sack show up everyone in the end. I cannot believe we have spent a whole evening arguing about a fictional book."

"Well, uh, that's sort of what I do. For a living. You know."

She gave her head a small shake. "Okay, now Mr. Professor of Theoretical Literature, I will go sit in your living room on your Prairie Arts and Crafts sofa which I like very much and will take another glass of this red wine, and I will read the rest of your manuscript and examine your theories, having the advantage of now being an expert on Mr. Berkeley's poisoned chocolates case."

He put away a few of the dishes and then joined her in the living room, sitting across from her on the other sofa. He thought briefly of Mary's admonition to play jazz for her, but thought it would seem silly and affected for him to start playing the piano at that moment and was afraid it might interrupt her concentration. He picked up his still barely touched cryptic puzzle instead. After a few minutes she glanced up. "What is that you are doing?"

"Oh, it's one of these hellacious cryptic crossword puzzles."

"What is cryptic?"

"Well, instead of just having a straight definition of the word, the clue is made up of two parts. One part is the dictionary definition. But the second part can be any number of things, like an anagram, or a rebus that spells out the word. And the sneaky part is that the whole clue is written as one sentence in a way that deliberately obscures which part is which. Like here's one. 'Roscoe, unfair player, loses head.' Six letters. And the answer is 'heater.'"

"That sounds absurd."

"No. The dictionary definition part, you see, is 'Roscoe,' which is gangster slang for a gun. And then 'unfair player loses head'— 'loses head' probably means that you drop the first letter—so, you see, unfair player is 'cheater,' and you drop the c off of 'cheater' and you get 'heater.' Which is also gangster slang for a gun."

"Well, I would not be so good at this since I am not such an expert on American gangster slangs. Though I am good at anagrams, I know."

"Well, usually an anagram is clued by a word like 'changed' or 'wild' or 'crooked.' Something like that. Here's one I've been hitting my head against just now. 'Poet composed sonnet about New York.' Eight letters."

Anika went back to reading the manuscript. "Tennyson," she said after a few seconds' pause.

Ted stared at her. "How did you get that."

"Well, 'composed sonnet' must mean an anagram of 'sonnet,' yes? Like you just told me. And that's six letters, so then 'about New York' must mean you put those letters somewhere around the letters NY, to make eight letters. And so 'poet' is the dictionary definition. So Tennyson."

"Jesus Christ."

"So, and while we are speaking of sonnets, why have you included this pretty little octave in your serious account of investigative researches? And where is the sestet that goes with it?"

His eyes widened in a momentary panic. "Oh, shit. I mean, I didn't mean to leave that in there. I guess you must have taken poetry for physicists," he nervously laughed; she, unconcerned by his discomfort, joined in with a more honest laugh. "Look, it's really stupid. In *Gaudy Night,* one of the Dorothy Sayers stories, Harriet Vane writes a sonnet and so I was thinking about that. And I was thinking about what you had said about me, and why I went into this line of work, and how I like to work with my hands and make things. And I realized it had been about fifteen years since I'd ever tried even making a poem of my own. And that was as far as I got. It's really dreadful, isn't it?"

"And what was her sonnet about?" she replied, ignoring his question. "Harriet Vane's?"

"Oh, it was about finding peace in the scholarly pursuit, escaping from the frenzy of life at the quiet center of the academic life. And she actually writes just the octave, and then Lord Peter finds it and finishes it and leaves his ending for her to find. And his sestet very cleverly mocks her search for peace, using her own images to point out that only a furiously spinning top can maintain its balance at the quiet center. So I guess I'm continuing our role reversal, aren't I? Writing the octave of a bad sonnet and leaving it for you to find. The anti-Lord Peter strikes again."

She smiled and shrugged and went back to the manuscript. He drifted out to finish cleaning up the kitchen. A half hour later she was at the door of the kitchen with her coat on. "Ted, my duty is with my tyrannical cat. Thank you for a lovely dinner and a lovely evening. I am now an expert on detective fiction and cryptic puzzles and bad poetry. I could do your job, yes?"

"I'm sure you could."

"Well, don't worry—I don't want it. Seriously, I have read your list of the facts and your amazing solutions. I think they are all wrong, but I want to think about this some more. There is a lot that is very creepy here, you know."

"Yes. I know," he sighed.

"Good night." Once again she gave him a very definite yet at the same time almost meaningless kiss full on the lips, and was gone.

He went to the living room. Tyrone was fast asleep on the sofa, snoring loudly.

On the coffee table he saw the sheet with his poem sitting on top of the folder.

Only it had grown a sestet, written in a firm hand in blue ink with no cross-outs or changes. "Goddamn," he said out loud and picked it up.

To reach that view I climbed the tower stair:
Forest, not trees; field, not grass; beach, not sand—
To see the whole, to grasp, to understand
What lower men did not dare think was there.
To count each blade, each grain; to strip twigs bare—
I might as well have stayed earthen bound and
Spared myself the climb, keeping with the band
Of slugs, who do not know, and do not care.

But he who would love must come back to ground
Facing the roughness of beauty and youth.
The distant view, the soft echoing sound
Are but a respite from the closer truth.

Once is enough up the precarious wall
Then never more fear, to never more fall.

Well, her use of meter wasn't so good, he thought petulantly; then at once felt foolish for being so juvenilely petty and competitive. But God, she had handled the turn of the sonnet just right: reversing his feelings of freedom and lofty perspective into escapism and posturing, his contempt for the ground below into an unwillingness to face truth and feeling—and love. He had been airily insisting that beauty is destroyed by messing with the ugly details. But here she was preaching the gospel of love and truth, beauty and logic; dismissing his airy theorizing as little more than adolescent folly: perhaps even timidity, masquerading as intellectual superiority, but fooling no one.

✠ 14.

Gilpin cancelled his classes for the rest of the week and stayed home and reread all of the Dorothy Sayers novels and several of Agatha Christie's and Dashiell Hammet's, taking breaks only to take Tyrone for a walk and eat leftover guacamole and enchiladas out of the serving dish while standing in front of the refrigerator. The phone rang a few times but he ignored it.

He lay on the sofa most of the day as he read, wearing the same shorts and a T-shirt he had worn to bed the night before, pulling on a pair of jeans and sneakers only when he went out with Tyrone. By nightfall on Wednesday, no closer to making sense of any of it than when he had begun, a gloom that felt like a physical weight bore down on him. He roused himself just before going to bed to play his phone messages: four calls from a woman who sounded eerily like his mother, wondering why he hadn't renewed his season subscription to the Lawless Opera and reminding him it wasn't too late, and then one from Mary, whose chirpily facetious tone made him briefly smile in spite of everything.

"Hello, stud muffin. Hope you're following my advice. Hey. You're a professor of English. Is this a sentence even? I am quoting from the newest addition to our law school website. Ready? 'AttorneysatLaw(less)'—that's all one word, of course, with no spaces but with parentheses around the 'less.' Get it? Anyway. 'AttorneysatLaw(less) is a new synergistic dynamically coordinated approach that actualizes the vision of integrating lawyering skills with a holistic amalgamation of experiential learning and traditional legal theory via the leveraging of our Centers of Excellence.'" She abruptly dropped the wise-guy manner. "Alright, just trying to interject a little levity. Ha ha ha. I mean, I didn't make that up—that's really what our fuckhead dean put on the website. But look, seriously. I've been hearing some weird rumors. And if you think you need a lawyer, don't screw around, okay? Give me a call if I can help put you in touch with someone. Alright? I hope you're okay. Really. Bye."

On Thursday afternoon he pulled himself together enough to feel he had to do something to get a grip on things, and slightly astonished himself by calling Wendy, Shalaby, Dr. John Doe, and several other colleagues from the music and art history departments to invite them to a dinner party on Friday. He called Mary, dodging her questions about both the police and Anika, but asking her to come too and as a special favor to him deflect the conversation away if it started to veer towards Mfuka's and Eric's deaths.

He wondered if he was doing it just as an excuse to see Anika again; but he invited her, too, and she sounded happy to come. It was a relief anyway to be doing something ordinary, maybe lift the oppressive spirits that had beset the department. He of course was unable to reach Shalaby, who never answered his phone; he'd knock on his door in the morning and ask him.

He had just gotten off the phone with Anika when it rang.

"Ah, Professor Gilpin," said a deep baritone. "So much has transpired since our last encounter. I wonder if you have any news for me, however?"

"Uh, who is this please?"

"This is—'G.', Professor Gilpin."

"Oh yes. Of course. Look—do you know what's been going on here? I mean two of my colleagues are dead. And not to mention one is still missing."

"Yes, most lamentable. But it did occur to me that a man of your considerable resources, Professor Gilpin—intellect, acuity, perspicacity, familiarity with the crime genre—could perhaps discern some revealing patterns even in these distressing events? Some fleeting shadow that upon closer examination would reveal itself to be the penumbra of that celestial object, if we might call it that, upon which I have so firmly set my sights?"

"No, I haven't figured out anything. Look, please can't you tell me what this manuscript is. What it's about. I'm sure if you told me that, I could—I could do a better job finding it. I can't help feeling it's the key to this whole thing."

The fat man chuckled. "Professor Gilpin, I had observed on the occasion of our most enjoyable meeting that you are a man without guile, but I see I must revise that assessment." He chuckled again, a sound of deep appreciation of a fine jest. "No, Professor Gilpin, I am a man of discretion. I am a patient man. One does not get where I am in life without those qualities. Well, if you do—*figure out* anything, I am sure you will tell me? But I remain convinced, Professor Gilpin, that if you can find where Professor Glantz is, you will find the key to *my* little mystery as well. Au revoir, professor. Until we speak again."

"Wait—" Gilpin began, but the connection was already broken.

He lay back on the sofa and tried to get his mind back to the novel he was reading but a few minutes later a knocking at the back door sent Tyrone into a tirade of barking. Gilpin quickly pulled on his trousers and made his way into the kitchen.

The police sergeant was standing imperturbably on his steps. He was by himself this time. "Sorry to bother you, again, professor, but I'm, afraid that's my job. Bothering people. How's the pooch doing?" he asked as Tyrone sniffed about his ankles. "Mind if I come in for a few minutes? And talk to you about an idea I had?"

Gilpin reluctantly led the policeman into his living room.

"You know, professor, we found a cell phone in the lagoon," the sergeant said as he sank into the chair. "Its serial number has been traced to you."

"Oh, uh, yes. I, well, got so mad at the 911 operator that I threw it in there."

"Uh huh. I see. You know professor, what's really bothered me about this case all along? I mean aside from this business you pointed out to me the other day of the way whoever is doing this seems to be copying things right out of detective stories?"

Gilpin shook his head.

"What bothers me, professor, is there's too much evidence. You know, real crimes are never like that. In fact, I'll let you in a little secret, professor. Real criminals are stupid. In fact, real criminal are incredibly stupid. Next to your typical criminal, I'm Einstein, and I'm no Einstein, if you see what I mean. You see, real criminals aren't anything like the criminals in mystery stories. I mean sure there's the clever sickos who get the big attention from the media, the serial wackos. But you know, professor, most criminals are just pathetic and dumb. You don't have to be Sherlock Holmes to catch them—they practically catch themselves. They get drunk, and their old lady starts yelling at them, so one of them sticks a bread knife into the other.

"Or they break into an apartment to rob somebody and come away with $23 in singles and loose change and an old color TV that doesn't even work anymore and then they get scared and shoot somebody who comes by at the wrong time. And then they brag about it to their friends, and their friends drop a nickel on them, and there's no mystery about it because there's a couple of big, fat, obvious things that tie them to the crime. Like they've still got the TV set that doesn't work sitting in their house. Or the security camera picked 'em up right at the scene of the crime, and there they are in living color.

"So, professor, I'm just a dumb cop like I told you, but sometimes something starts bothering me and this was one of those somethings. And I started wondering if this thing that was bothering me—namely why there were so many clues in these two cases—had something to do with the reason why someone would want to copy crimes out of a detective storybook in the first place. Just an idea, you understand, professor.

"And you know, professor, one of the things I decided I might do as long as this idea was bothering me was to read the paper you wrote you told me about." He pulled out a copy of Gilpin's Dorothy Sayers article. It was covered with yellow highlighter and underlining. "So I read it. And I even looked up some of the references you had. In your footnotes."

"Really?" Gilpin asked uneasily.

"Yeah. I went to the library. They were really very helpful there." A tone of slight wonderment entered his voice. "Real nice. I mean, I just went in there and they didn't know me from Adam and I sure didn't know them, but I must have had three librarians just about fighting over which one would get to help me. And the place was practically deserted. Don't students ever use the library? I thought that's what a library at a university was for."

"Uh, well, not so much anymore. Students tend to, well, just look things up on the Internet. It's kind of hard to get them to read a real book, to be honest with you, these days."

"Is that a fact?" He chewed the side of his mouth. "How much they charge for tuition here these days, professor?"

"I think it's about forty-five thousand dollars—that's tuition, room, and board. A year."

The cop whistled. "You know, I think if I was paying forty-five thousand a year to send my daughter here, I'd want her to read a book now and then. But anyway, like I was saying, they were real nice there in the library. And they found me this one book I was especially looking for that you had listed in one of your footnotes. It's called *Who Killed Roger Ackroyd*. By Pierre Bayard. You know that book, professor?"

"Yes, of course. It's a quite penetrating analysis of the structure of the detective novel."

"Well, that may be, but to be honest with you professor, I'll tell you I had a hard time getting through it at first. I had to keep looking up the words in it. Like hermeneutics—that how you say it?"

"Hermeneutics. Right."

"Yeah, well, it was funny about that word, in particular, you know, because I'd look it up in the dictionary, then it was like I'd right away forget what it means and have to look it up again the next time I saw it. Anyway, professor, when I got through this book, at first I thought this guy Bayard was just a show-off. That all he was doing was saying, hey look how smart I am, I can come up with a better solution to an Agatha Christie than Agatha Christie did. But then I read it again. And you know what I think he was saying?"

"No. I mean, well I think *I* know what he was saying. But what are you saying he was saying."

"Well, I'll tell you. Maybe I'm wrong here, because like I say I'm not a professor like you, but I think he was saying that really *anybody* could have come up with another solution to an Agatha Christie. In fact, he was saying that anybody can *always* come up with another solution—I mean when you're dealing with a detective story—I mean when it's a detective story like you find in books, not the ones in real life, with real criminals. The stupid ones I was telling you about." The sergeant leaned back and folded his hands over his belly, giving Gilpin an impassive look like a poker player who had just raised a bet.

"Well, I guess I'd agree with that. Point of view is critical to giving a text meaning."

"Well is that it professor? Because I thought he was saying something a little different. I thought he was saying there's really two parts of a detective story. The first part is supposed to keep the reader guessing. So the writer throws all kinds of fake clues and distractions at the reader. Like, sometimes the culprit is disguised by making him somebody you'd never think of as a murderer—like a doctor, or a priest, or a cop, or even the person who's telling the story. Like what happens in *The Murder of*

Roger Ackroyd. I mean the way Agatha Christie wrote it. Not the way this guy Bayard re-solved it."

"The unreliable narrator."

"Unreliable narrator. Is that what you call it?"

Gilpin nodded.

"I gotta remember that. That's good. Unreliable narrator. He's the guy telling the story, but he doesn't tell us the whole truth. You can't rely on what he's saying. That's good."

The cop stopped, looked down, and scratched behind his ear.

"You know, professor," he continued, "I figured I had to go and read the original *Murder of Roger Ackroyd,* too, after reading *Who Killed Roger Ackroyd.* They helped me find that at the library, too. It seemed kind of funny to me that a university would have a bunch of Agatha Christies. But then I guess there are professors like you and this Bayard guy who write serious articles about this stuff, so they have to have 'em, right? But what's also funny, what with you mentioning to me how all the things that have been happening seem to be someone copying a crime novel, is that you didn't mention this other connection."

Gilpin looked away uneasily and cleared his throat but said nothing.

The sound of a ticking clock on the mantle and the dog's gentle snoring filled the silence for a half a minute while the sergeant waited, the same expressionless look on his face. "Well, I mean I see what you're saying about Professor Bariki's death and the Dorothy Sayers *Have His Carcase* book, his throat being cut and all," he continued, "but you didn't mention that some of the things about it also seem kind of close to what happens in *The Murder of Roger Ackroyd.* I mean, in that story, the narrator—the 'unreliable narrator,' but he's telling the truth about this one—gets a phone call bringing him to the scene of the crime. Only the person the call is supposed to be from says he didn't make the call. Anyway, it's a funny coincidence, isn't it?"

Gilpin again did not reply, but the cop seemed not to notice or care and went right on without a pause this time. "So anyway, to get back to what I was saying before, Bayard says in his book that sometimes the murderer is disguised by making him a doctor or a priest or someone respectable. And sometimes he's disguised by making him look like he's going to be a victim himself. Like he gets threatening letters. And so naturally you don't think he could be the one who's doing it. And then Bayard says another way the writer keeps you guessing is he throws in all kinds of distractions. He calls attention to funny coincidences, or strange things that happen. And after a while you start thinking anybody could be the murderer. So that's the first part of the book. But then in the second part of the book the author has to somehow get rid of all these possibilities and narrow it down to just one culprit.

"And here's the thing where I thought Bayard was pretty on the ball, when I went back and read it the second time. He says that for any mystery story to work in the first part—to keep the reader guessing—the writer's got to throw in so many possibilities that he *never* can really get rid of them all by the end of the story. And so even though the detective at the end announces he's found the murderer, and he comes up with some reasons to explain it, the truth is anybody else who put their mind to it could come along after the book is over and drive a truck right through the detective's case.

"And you know what that got me thinking, professor? I was thinking. Maybe if somebody out there was really smart like this Bayard and say he wanted to commit a real murder. And say he's read a lot of detective stories, and read a lot of books like this Bayard book which—what was that you said, professor, analyzes the structure of the detective story?

"And so maybe he realizes a perfect way to cover his tracks is to commit a murder right out of a detective story. Because if he's following the script of a detective story, he's going to be doing exactly what the writer does. He's going to be like a detective-story writer himself, except in real life. He's going to be leaving so many

false leads and disguises and distractions that no solution—
especially no solution that some dumb cop, say, might come up
with—is ever going to be the only one that anyone *could* come up
with. There's going to be all of these left over bits and pieces that
someone else could always come along and put together in some
completely different way. Like I said, it's like the murderer is writing one of these detective stories, except it's real life."

The cop paused and squinted his eyes ever so slightly. "I mean
it makes you think, doesn't it, professor?"

"Look, sergeant, I mean—and I'm really not just saying this, but
that's really very insightful. I mean you've done more reading than
my students ever do and you've put your finger on something
very—perceptive."

The sergeant looked as pleased as a schoolboy who was called
on in class and had given the right answer.

"But if you're trying to suggest by all of this that I had anything
to do with any of these deaths of my colleagues, or with the threatening letters, or Julie Glantz's disappearance, that's just crazy. I
mean these are my friends. I mean I've had threatening messages
too. And whoever is doing this is obviously trying to plant clues
that get me in trouble. And for crissake, what could possibly be
my motive, anyway?"

The sergeant smiled politely. "You know, professor, motive is
another thing right out of detective stories that doesn't have much
to do with real detective work. I can tell you, professor, cops don't
sit around like Sherlock Holmes or—what's his name, Hercule
Poy-rot figuring out motives. When you find who did it, the motive comes along by itself. And usually, it's pretty simple. Anger.
Jealousy. Money. Nut case."

Gilpin thought for a minute and fingered a hole in the knee of
his jeans. "You know, there's a lot in what you said. I mean about
why someone would want to pattern a real crime on the text of a
detective novel. But now that I'm thinking about it, there's still a
lot of ways these crimes—or whatever they are, I mean we still

don't know that they're not an accident and a suicide, right? I mean for sure?—but there's a lot ways these don't follow the classic rules of the detective story at all."

"How do you figure that, professor?"

"Well, back in 1928, there was a famous American detective story writer, S. S. Van Dine—that was actually the pseudonym he published most of his stories under—and he published a list of twenty rules for detective stories." Gilpin had automatically fallen into the tone of lecturing to a class.

"Yeah, Bayard mentions him in his book, right?"

"Uh, yes, I think so." The sergeant again looked pleased with himself. Gilpin couldn't help thinking he wished he had a class full of students like him. "Some of the rules of course are not ones that fit one way or another into your theory because they're just about the structure of the writing. Things like, oh, you can't have long descriptive passages. Or a love interest." Gilpin cleared his throat. "Um, or also you can't use supernatural explanations, or have the murderer use a poison that's unknown to science. And there can only be one detective, and he has to actually solve the crime at the end, and it can't turn out to be an accident or suicide. And you can't have the butler do it, or some minor character. And he also lists a whole bunch of hackneyed tricks you can't use anymore. Like the old Sherlock Holmes dog that didn't bark in the night, or matching the cigarette ash left at the scene of the crime, or the detective decoding a secret message, or having the murderer turn out to be the twin of the chief suspect.

"But his most important rules are that all of the relevant clues have to be in plain sight, so the reader *could* have figured out the solution himself—if he were as clever as the detective. And the author can't play any tricks on the reader that the criminal himself doesn't play on the detective. But it seems to me what's happening here is nothing but tricks and hiding things with the aim of deliberately misleading the police. And everyone else."

"You know, professor, I read that part in Bayard's book,

where he talks about these rule about having the clues in plain sight. But, at least the way I look at it, he was saying that even though the real clues *are* out there in plain sight, at the same time they're disguised by a whole lot of other clues. I mean isn't that what he's saying—just because the important clues are out there in plain sight, the reader doesn't necessarily know which ones he's supposed to pay attention to. Right? So that, to me anyway, professor, seems to back up what I'm saying."

Gilpin laughed a bit self-consciously. "You know, sergeant, maybe I could have you come in as a guest lecturer if I offer that class again."

"I don't know, professor. Those students—they seem like they'd be a tough audience. You should see what I have to deal with on Saturday nights. Hell, any night, the way these students drink—like fishes. But I think I'll stick with my job. It's not the nicest job in the world, but it's about my speed. Really nice home you've got here, professor," he said looking around the living room and pulling his large frame to his feet. "Well, give me a call anytime if you have any information. Or if something occurs to you you want to share with us. Or get off your conscience. You will do that, professor?"

Gilpin nodded. The cop headed back for the door, then said as if an afterthought. "Say, professor. I meant to ask you. Is this yours?" He pulled an evidence bag from his pocket and handed it to Gilpin. In it was a door key.

"Well, it looks like the keys to the offices in Trojan Hall. He reached into his pocket and pulled out a small ring of keys. "No, mine is right here."

"Oh. Well, just wondering."

"Why, what is that?"

"Oh, it's a key to Professor Shalaby's office. We found it in the pond. Right next to where we found your cell phone. Well, have a nice day, professor. And don't forget to call if anything occurs to you.

✤ 15.

A pink drawstring gift bag was sitting on the dark oak bench in the hallway outside his office when Gilpin finally stopped in in the morning. He picked it up and carried it into his office.

Taped to the bag was a card with a picture of a mournful looking baby seal and the words "I'm sooooooo sorry" on the front. He reluctantly opened the card. "Dear professor Gilpin," was written in curvy handwriting with a pink felt pen. "I'm sooooo sorry I didn't get my assignment in on time. This is a <u>really</u> <u>really</u> stressful time for me and it's <u>really</u> important I get an A in this class for my GPA. But I don't think it was fair that we didn't know ahead of time how much time it would take. And I don't see that I should give a 'strongly agree' on the student evaluation for 'this course is conducted in an atmosphere of mutual tolerance, courtesy, and respect' when things aren't fair like this. Tiffany." The "i" in "Tiffany" had a large circle over it. He rolled his eyes. In the bag was a box of Belgian chocolates. The blend of cringing apologies, threats, and attempted bribery was about par for the course, he thought.

He left the box of chocolates on his desk and walked down the hall to Shalaby's office.

Ignoring the "Do Not Disturb" sign he boldly knocked on the door. On the fourth try a furious voice answered from within. "Do you have a problem with reading? Is the sign somehow unclear? Is it the 'do,' the 'not,' or the 'disturb' that is perhaps unclear? I am fascinated. Please tell me."

"Douad. It's Ted. Sorry to bother you—can I talk to you for just a second?"

The sound of a door chain being impatiently slid loose and falling against the jamb was followed by the door flying open. A small cloud of cigarette smoke poured out. Ted choked slightly.

It was practically pitch-black in the office. The venetian blinds over the window were shut tight and only a small slit of light crept in over the top. A small desk lamp and the fluorescent glow from the computer screen were the only other sources of light in the room.

"Douad," Ted said when he recovered, "I'm having a dinner party tonight. For everyone in the department. To try to, well—well, everyone's been at everyone's throats, and with all of these terrible things, with Eric, and Mfuka, I just thought maybe we ought to pull together a bit and try to bury all the hatchets. And so please come. Okay?"

Shalaby still looked angry. "So, you're a candidate for the Nobel Peace Prize? Like those other great war criminals—Henry Kissinger? And Begin?"

"Look, please Douad."

"I thought you would not want a typical Jew-hating Arab in your home."

Gilpin was stunned for second. "Jesus, Douad, you can't possibly believe I was the one who said that."

"Alright. I'll come."

"Okay, that's more like it. Seven o'clock. Okay?" He found his eyes glancing over to where he remembered the commando knife had once sat on the side of Shalaby's desk. Through the gloom and the haze of cigarette smoke he noticed a new item he hadn't seen before. It resembled a dart, with a menacingly sharp point at the front and fins on the back, except that it was huge, two feet long, an inch in diameter. "What on earth is that thing, Douad?"

"That is an M829 kinetic energy penetrator. The American soldiers in Iraq called it the 'magic bullet.' It is fired from an

American tank gun and when it strikes a tank or other vehicle it causes large pieces of hot metal from the inside of the vehicle to spall off and kill or simply maim everyone inside with crippling injuries. And do you know why it is 'magic'?"

"Uh, no, Douad. No. I don't."

"It is made of what the American military calls 'depleted' uranium. They claim, of course, that it is not radioactive or harmful. But thousands of Iraqi babies have cancer. Thousands of women in Kosovo have mysterious illness. It is a weapon of genocide, not warfare."

"Uh. Okay, Douad. But geez, is it safe to have that thing in here? I mean if it really is radioactive? Or toxic?"

"I am not afraid of taking personal risks to expose the truth about the American military-industrial war of genocide that is being waged under the name of the so-called 'war on terror.'"

"Yeah, but what about the rest of us?"

Shalaby just glowered.

"Right. Okay—well—see you tonight, Douad. Oh, Douad. You don't have any idea where Julie is, or what happened to her, do you?"

"Perhaps *she* is the Arab-hating Jew who complains about Jew-hating Arabs? No. I don't know. I don't care."

Gilpin thought for someone who was sensitive about being accused of being an anti-Semite, Shalaby had a strange way of defending himself.

As he left the office early that afternoon, he decided the party would need higher-octane stimulus than the cheap Chilean red that had somehow become the standard for academic dinner parties. He stopped in at the liquor store and tried to remember the weird brand of gin Travis had always liked. Something with rose petals and cucumbers in the flavor—Jesus.

He searched the shelves and finally found it. The label said it was made in Glasgow. Second prize was no doubt two bottles of gin made in Glasgow; but he got it anyway, along with a boxed set of a dozen traditional martini glasses that were on special. They were going to need it tonight.

At the local upscale grocery store he discovered that since the last time he'd been there, the week before, they had replaced one entire aisle with nothing but water, and another with only olive oil. A few young mothers with short haircuts, clad in exercise clothes, obliviously ignoring shrieking toddlers who were running up and down the aisle, were chatting with a sharply dressed young man who was standing behind a table with a sign that announced blasamic vinegar tasting 3-5 p.m.

Gilpin picked up a leg of lamb, spinach, chickpeas, ginger, garlic, basmati rice, papadams, and eight bottles of Chilean red. And a bag of dog food. In the water aisle his eyes started to glaze over, and he finally grabbed four large bottles closest to him and fled to the checkout.

He had the lamb boned, cubed, and marinating in a puree of the garlic, ginger, and spices and the spinach and chickpea dishes simmering on the low burners when Anika arrived. She was early; she brought flowers; she was back to wearing her standard jeans and white tee but she had made a tiny, perfect braid in her hair that ran along one side on the top of her head. It again made him think of a Renaissance portrait. She always seemed so unselfconscious of her looks that he found himself surprised, almost astonished by the little things she did now and then to accentuate her appearance; no different from what all women did, but so at odds with the determinedly natural way she carried herself.

The Scottie, having remembered how successful his attention-getting routine had been last time, again interrupted his greeting of her by sliding halfway across the kitchen floor into Anika's legs. This time he waited until she had finished greeting the dog and then kissed her on each cheek. "So you are again being Ted Gilpin master chef," she said looking around at his dinner preparations, "leaving the maidens of the district breathless with your culinary prowess in the kitchen?"

"You know, you don't make it easy being a guy these days." He tried to say it as a joke but it came out a bit defensive and self-pitying. A picture of Eeyore the donkey flashed into his mind: drooping head, sagging ears, missing tail.

"Oh. Poor guys," she said.

"No, but really. I keep seeing these articles about how women want men to be all sensitive and to not be afraid of defying gender stereotypes and the when we do those things you make fun of us for not being macho enough. We can't win."

"No, I am not making fun of you for cooking. I am making fun of you for cooking as a competitive sport. That is exactly the usual male approach to everything."

"No, that's unfair, too. I'm only competing against myself. It's just the way to get the job the done. You know, get the blood flowing. Like, well, a bull moose charging into a tree."

"Yes, exactly. And I think I could make you a graph—a real graph that is 100 percent scientifically valid in this case—that would show a precise correlation between a bull moose's blood testosterone level and how many times a minute he charges into a tree. And injures his head."

They were interrupted by the simultaneous arrival of Mary, Wendy Heatherton, and Dr. John Doe and his wife. Ursula Doe, whom he had met only a few times before, was an amateur interior decorator and a professional Texan. Dr. John Doe had started to mumble what he apparently thought would be some appropriate remarks about Eric and Mfuka but was almost immediately interrupted by his wife.

"Real nahce little place ya got here, Ted," she brayed. "Course, needs a few touches here and there. Come on, Ted, and we'll fix it up real nahce for ya. Let me have the grand tour." Ted reluctantly found himself being dragged through his own house and bombarded with a nonstop stream of decorating commands by a voice that reminded him of a semitrailer putting on its brakes. "Okay, what we're gonna do here, Tay-ed, is put up a few wall-hangings," she was saying in the living room. "With a touch a Asian influence. That's what I like. And we're gonna put a roof deck on this space yer wastin' up there now. Now, we need to re-*ad*-just the Feng Shui in hair. An' add some nahce Tuscan colors."

He finally managed to steer her back to the kitchen where everyone else still was standing around. They had been since joined by all of the other guests except for Shalaby. Dr. John Doe was looking a bit puzzled. Anika had been cornered by a particularly gay art historian who, Ted noticed, always monopolized the prettiest women at parties.

Wendy was scowling at the lamb and saying something about animal rights and artificial hormones and chemicals. Mary was alertly following the mission Ted had assigned her of nipping in the bud any talk about the recent tragedies and changing the conversation to innocuous topics. She had already distracted Dr. John Doe twice more as he tried to deliver his obviously prepared appropriate remarks; now he tried again, but this time it was Wendy, to Gilpin's astonishment—could he be hearing this right?—who seemed to have interrupted him to put in a claim to Bariki's corner office.

He thought he'd better not waste any more time before getting some drinks into his guests. He quickly mixed a pitcher of martinis and dispensed them while herding everyone into the living room. Everyone, he was relieved to see, took one, except for Dr. John Doe, who, as always, asked for a sparkling water with lime.

He went back to the kitchen to get the lamb started cooking. Bits of academic shop talk drifted in: the universal anodyne of intellectuals in the face of emotional trauma.

"...announcement they sent out didn't say anything except that they were starting a search for a new department chair, didn't even bother mentioning that the reason was someone walked into the conference room and there was the *current* department chair right on the conference room table giving it to a freshman...of course the hard part isn't ever detecting students' plagiarism, it's proving it...talk about going out with a bang...had all these references to unpublished theses from the Sorbonne and papers at the University of Texas archives, and he started crying when I confronted him with it...doesn't have German or French, ridiculous...third time she got pregnant just to delay her tenure decision...he hadn't been allowed to teach a class for seven years because of the sexual harassment complaints, but Humphreys was demanding I vote for him for chair...never could figure out why he got that office, but then it turned out *he* was the one who'd been bonking the provost all that time...no, the *best* place to stay in Paris..."

Ted kept popping into the living room to refill the martini glasses while he finished preparing the dinner. Each time he came in, Mary made increasingly insistent gestures towards the piano, but he kept giving what he hoped was a subtle shake of his head to warn her off. Things on the whole seemed to be progressing satisfactorily. Shalaby still hadn't arrived. The Scottie circulated affably among the guests, cadging pieces of papadums and occasionally leaping onto a sofa for a closer inspection of one or another of the visitors.

He was just stirring a final smarting dose of garam masala into the lamb when Mary appeared in the kitchen doorway. "Ted, I just have two things to say to you, you worm. First, she is absolutely gorgeous and wonderful and brilliant, and second if you do not get your sorry ass down in front of that piano and play one Fats Waller tune this instant, I will annihilate you."

Before he could reply she turned on her heels and Ted turned bright red as he heard her announce from the next room in a commanding, and only slightly inebriated, voice, "Ladies and gentleman, it is my great pleasure now to introduce to you on the piano, live from the Papadum Room high above the beautiful waters of Lake Erie, our very own sultan of syncopation and duke of deconstruction, that perspicacious piano pounder himself...Mr. Ted Gilpin." A hail of facetious applause and hoots followed.

Acceding to the inevitable, Ted decided he might as well play it for maximum ham value and strode into the living room, gave a deep bow, and was relieved when nearly all the guests then proceeded to immediately ignore him and resume their conversations at maximum volume as he sat down at the piano and launched into the slow opening bars of "Waiting at the End of the Road."

A simple Irving Berlin tune that Fats Waller had liked to play around with so much he had once recorded it four times in a single session: Gilpin finished the lyrical, meandering sixteen bar statement of the verse, taking it much more freely and rubato than Waller ever did, then swung into a Waller-like stride bass for the chorus, and soon was lost in the tune and variations, choosing to keep it more restrained and less flashy in the right hand than he usually did until he came to the last chorus, then brought it a stomping close with heavily accented chords outlining the melody for one rousing refrain.

More exaggerated applause and hoots; Ted stood up and bowed deeply again, then hoping to cover the embarrassment he knew was showing through, cupped his hands around his mouth shouted, "Let's eat!"

He caught Anika's slightly arch look directed at him, the same slightly amused surprise, lifted eyebrows and faint smile, he had seen on her face at the Blue Olive.

As they entered the dining room he managed to guide Anika to the place next to him; on her other side the gay art historian firmly attached himself, still regaling her with the story of his career. Wendy grabbed the seat on Ted's other side with a glint in her eye.

Uh oh, he thought. She had seemed to have loosened up a bit from the last time he had been in the living room, but now he was worried she had slipped past the affable drunk stage and into something more dangerous. "Didn't you say Douad was coming?" she asked with an excessively sweet tone of voice that increased his guard.

"Yes. I guess he's late."

"Profound tautological insight, Ted. As always." Her saccharine smile changed to a sneer. "Good old Douad. When I first came here, he told me he 'didn't have time to waste' getting to know faculty members without tenure, because they would only be here a year or two." She filled up her wine glass.

Her unpleasant reminiscences were interrupted by the arrival of Shalaby himself. He took the vacant chair half way down the table on the side opposite Anika.

"So," Wendy said in a commanding voice at that moment, looking right at Anika. She managed to get even the art historian to break his conversational stride. "I'm fascinated to know what a real woman physicist thinks about *l'affaire Summers.* I mean, of course, a real physicist who is a woman. Apparently even Ted here has been able to figure out that you're a real woman. Though of course we always had some questions about Ted," she said sweetly. "I'd been thinking of taking bets about whether he'd end up with a cute blonde or a big black guy first. So, I guess it turns out there must have been a shortage of big black guys. So anyway, *Anika,* what about it? Women in physics. *Why* so few? Natural inability? Discrimination? Acculturation?"

Wendy was clearly blotto, but did not betray it in any way so obvious as slurring her words. If anything, it was the fact that she was speaking with inordinate precision that was the indicator she was exceedingly drunk.

Luckily a loud conversation was continuing unabated at the other end of the table as Ursula Doe was going on about the latest trends in something she kept calling "furniture therapy," so the discomfort Wendy had delighted in creating was for the moment confined to Ted, Anika, and the art historian.

Dr. John Doe, sitting next to Wendy, formed a sort of vacuous buffer zone that so far kept the conflagration from spreading; he had said almost nothing the whole evening, and was still smiling slightly and looking a bit lost.

On the opposite side of the table Mary had been valiantly

struggling to create a more active break by keeping up a backfire of questions to Ursula.

Anika had turned and listened with outward composure to Wendy's question. "I suspect it is not any one thing," she replied. "But we know girls do just as well if not better at math than boys in high school. Then at some point they do not go on to careers in math and science. So it is clearly not a lack of natural ability."

"And you? Have *you* been discriminated against?"

"I cannot say I have, but..."

Shalaby interrupted from down the table: the heat of Wendy's ire had now leapt over the firebreak of Dr. John Doe and was clearly threatening to give rise to a general inferno. Ted fidgeted nervously with his wine glass.

"I do not see why gender equality is something to be desired in physics," Shalaby was saying, loudly and angrily. "American physics is responsible for the greatest genocidal acts in human history. It is like fighting for more women to be represented among spouse abusers and sex offenders and Nazi concentration camp guards."

Anika looked at him placidly. "I think you know very little about physics."

"Oh. So the entire humanist critique is invalidated because we have not undergone the same indoctrination that produces this genocidal mindset in the first place."

"Criticism has to be based on knowledge and information to have any meaning," she replied. "And frankly, Dr. Shalaby, I think the sciences have far more claim to the humanist tradition today than the humanities do. In fact, the sciences *are* the real humanities today. We are actually the last holdouts of the humanist tradition, seeking knowledge and truth for its own sake, allowing that truth to speak for itself and take us wherever it goes, without fear and without political or religious agendas. Most physicists you will find are actually very apolitical. Whereas most humanists are so political that they allow their personal belief to skew their knowledge. Either that, or they treat the very idea of knowledge as a sort of intellectual joke."

"You think it is a joke, exposing the crimes of the Zionist occupiers?"

Wendy now started to bore in again but both Ted and Mary rushed to cut her off, both clearly intent on changing the subject. Then, fatally, each stopped to let the other to go first, and Wendy smoothly slipped into the gap.

"So, *Anika,* let's just say for the sake of argument that a woman physicist *didn't* have a body that would qualify her to, say, pose for the centerfold of *Physics Today* and have a bunch of dominant males drooling into their pocket protectors over her. How about *her?* Would *she* face discrimination in physics?"

Anika again ignored the sneer and offered a straight and composed reply. "I think the discrimination is more a matter of institutional culture. It is not that women are unwilling to work eighty hour weeks. There are plenty of women doctors, and lawyers, and businesspeople who do just that. But it takes a critical mass to change the atmosphere. Those were old-boy clubs, too, who made women feel unwelcome. And I think the lab culture in science is also very much a nerdy guy culture that does not appeal to women. But there is no reason one has to be a nerd to do science well."

There was another slight pause and Ted, desperately clutching at straws, started to tell the very long shaggy-dog joke that Billy Collins had incorporated into a poem which he had read the other day. It went on for about three minutes, and Ted soon realized that he could not remember the last time anyone had told a joke at a party. No one told jokes anymore.

He was aware that everyone was looking at him strangely, but he pressed on, feeling like he was digging himself into a deeper and deeper hole with each twist and turn of the interminable story.

It was about the miracle-working rabbi who claimed to be able to bring the dead back to life. He keeps trying to bring this one corpse back to life, reciting incantations, saying prayers, but there's not a flicker of life. Ted got to the punch line. "And so the rabbi shrugs his shoulders and says, 'Now that's what I call *dead.*'"

There was a deafening silence. Wendy said acidly, "Ted, does anyone actually need to explain to you that the so-called joke was nothing but an outmoded patriarchal device to permit men to dominate discourse while revealing nothing of themselves?"

"Hey, Ted," the art historian spoke up, garrulously and vinously. "What do *you* think is behind all this terrible business in D-CADS. Have we got some madman loose?" Ted had been hoping to avoid the topic altogether, but it was almost a relief compared to the way the conversation had been going. He gave as brief and cursory a reply as he felt he could. "Probably some student," the art historian was now saying. "They're all on antidepressants these days."

Ted seized the opportunity to start clearing the dinner plates and, he hoped, avoid being drawn into any further talk on the matter. As he was carrying a tray out to the kitchen he heard Shalaby starting to say, "It is obviously all a part of this same effort to create an atmosphere of intimidation—first these slanderous accusations, then the obvious ploy of using the knife taken from my office in an attempt to incriminate the victim..."

He got the bowl of poached pears he had prepared earlier out of the refrigerator and started to carry them in, then, almost as an afterthought, picked up the box of Belgian chocolates and brought them, too. Wendy, who had barely picked at the dinner, immediately commandeered the box, scrutinized the list of ingredients on the side, then opened it and started picking methodically through the first layer of chocolates.

Shalaby left a few minutes later. But it was close to one a.m. before the others finally had drained the rest of the wine, and with many false starts, finally got themselves out the door and into their cars and away.

Anika helped him carry in the last of the wine glasses and plates, and they were alone in the kitchen. He had drunk enough wine himself to lose some of his usual reticence but still not his usual self-consciousness.

"I'm sorry about that," he said sheepishly. "I mean those things Wendy and Douad were saying."

She shrugged. "Oh, I know better to take seriously what drunken academics say."

"Oh." He looked concerned.

"What?"

"Does that mean you're not taking seriously what I'm saying? I mean, my being an academic. And well not exactly drunken, but..."

She smiled at him.

He walked over to her and, standing before her, suddenly took both of her hands in his. "Anika. Oh, God. Well. Let's see, I guess first I'm going to apologize for being apologetic, then I'm going to be apologetic. Sorry—but you *know*, I just can't help it. So let me do it just this once."

"Wait, when you said just now you were sorry, was that the apology for being apologetic, or was that the being apologetic?" she asked, deadpan.

"Oh. That was I guess the apologizing for apologizing. About being apologetic. Which I haven't done yet."

"You are very funny when you have had a bit to drink. Okay, I will let you this time. Only." Her hands felt long and cool in his.

"Okay. I know guys don't go around saying things like this anymore—"

"Wait—is *this* the being apologetic?"

"Uh, yeah. *Now* I'm being apologetic. Before I was saying I was sorry that I was going to be apologetic."

"Okay. Please pardon the interruption. Do continue. Please. I'm listening. It's fascinating." She put on a face of pretended rapt concentration.

"Okay." He took a deep breath. "Well, anyway, I know guys don't say things like this anymore,—"

"Yes, you just said that. Oh, sorry. Forgive *me*. *Please* continue." She again struck an expression of innocent attention. She was taking inordinate pleasure in tormenting him.

"—but I think you're the most beautiful girl I've ever seen in my life."

"Well, Professor Gilpin, that is the prettiest thing you have said to me. I am glad to know you are not just interested in me for my brain."

"Well I've been looking for a chance to show you I wasn't."

"So show me."

✤ 16.

Unlike the week before when they had innocently shared his bed together, this night he slept a deep and utterly dreamless sleep. He was awaken early in the morning by the sensation of a tongue gently licking his ear. "God, Anika, I don't think I can keep—," he started to say, and half opened eyes. This time it was a mass of coarse, black fur he found himself staring into. He opened his eyes all the way and found he had his arm around the Scottie, who was lying between them, his head nestled between the two pillows. He gently picked up the dog and lowered him to the floor, then moved closer to Anika, and fell blissfully back to sleep.

It was almost noon when the ringing phone dragged him at last from bed. A brisk, professional voice he didn't recognize asked for him.

"*This* is Ted Gilpin," he replied.

"This is Dr. Martin at University Hospital. We have a Wendy Heatherton here. It's a slightly strange case, and we're running tests, but at first blush anyway it looks like food poisoning. I understand she was at your house last night for dinner, which is why I'm calling. Has anyone else who ate dinner with you become ill?"

"Ill? What would the symptoms be?" Gilpin asked, immediately feeling queasy.

"Oh, nausea, vomiting...headache...abdominal cramping, watery diarrhea." Gilpin started feeling worse and worse. "Fever, dizziness, muscle aches, blurred vision, bloody stool, mucous in the..."

Gilpin hastily cut him off. "No, I don't think so. I mean I'm all right. I think." He looked uneasily at Anika, who was still gently sleeping on her side. "Look, is Wendy okay?"

"I would say her condition is serious. We'd like to come and take some samples of the food you had to see if we can track this down. And we'd like to get contact information for your other guests. It's routine when there's a suspected case of foodborne illness, you understand."

"Yes, of course."

"Meanwhile, let me ask you—do you recall if there was anything Ms. Heatherton ate that you or the others didn't?"

He cast his mind over the dinner. Wendy hadn't eaten much, he remembered. Then a picture of her snarfing up the chocolates came into his mind. "Oh. Well, there were some chocolates. She ate a lot of those. I'm not sure anyone else had more than one or two, but I think she put away a lot. But, surely that couldn't...." His voice trailed off and he felt himself turning white. He gripped the phone as if for support. "Look, doctor, this couldn't be a, uh, case of poisoning. I mean some real poison?"

There was a surprised pause on the other end. "What makes you say that?"

"Oh, nothing. Really. I mean. Well, maybe I'm just feeling kind of paranoid. We've had two other deaths in my department this week and....Well, I'm imagining things I'm sure."

"Well, now that you mention it, there are some possible similarities to arsenic poisoning. It would be pretty unusual to see that. But we're running tests to cover all the possibilities we can think of. Now if you'll just see that nothing is disturbed from whatever food you have left over from last night, we'll have a technician come over to collect some samples. And someone will be calling to get the list of names and numbers of your other guests."

Anika had been awaken by the urgent tone in his voice when he had begun to ask about poison. She sat up and looked at him curiously. He rapidly filled in the story. "You know," he then added, his throat tightening as he spoke, "there's another Dorothy Sayers novel. *Strong Poison*. Harriet Vane's fiancé gets poisoned. By arsenic. They think she did it, but Lord Peter gets her off. And then of course there's also *The Poisoned Chocolates Case*. Which we talked about. The other night."

Anika said nothing. Then: "Chocolates." Then, abruptly: "I think I'm going to be sick."

She rushed past him to the bathroom and he heard her retching. After a few minutes she came out, her cheeks pale and her eyes bloodshot. "Anika," he said and started to touch her shoulder, but she moved quickly across the room, sat on the edge of the bed, and began gathering her clothes.

"I'd better go."

"No, wait." But she was already pulling on her jeans. "No, really. Stay. A little longer. Maybe I'd better take you to the clinic."

"I have to go feed my cat." She said it with an iciness that froze him.

"But if you're ill..."

"I am sure it was just psychosomatic. I did not eat any of the chocolates."

"Anika, what's going on."

"Nothing's 'going on.' I have to go feed my cat." He watched helplessly as she pulled her tee shirt over her head, flipped her hair out from the collar, gave it a few quick strokes with a brush she pulled from her bag, slipped her feet into her shoes, and started for the door.

"Anika. For God's sake. Didn't—well, didn't last night mean anything at all?"

"Last night was fine, thank you." She smiled a strangely mechanical smile. "Bye." And she was out the door.

He sat bewildered.

He called her home and office numbers every ten minutes for the next three hours, but there was no answer at either one.

The technician from the hospital came and took away samples of the last night's dinner and the remains of the box of chocolate. She poured out the dregs out of the wine bottles and dipped out a sample of the gin into a test tube using a pipette. She wore latex surgical gloves and said little.

When she was gone, he finally switched on his computer and sent Anika an email: "Please tell me what's going on. As the Pathan horse trader said to Kim, 'Speak a little plainer. All the world may tell lies save thou and I.' I love you."

He noticed a message in his inbox from Sarah Battell in the organ curator's shop. It had come Friday afternoon. "Hi Professor Gilpin," it began, "I tried to call you this afternoon but couldn't reach you. I found a package in the organ chamber with Julie Glantz's name on it. I know you had been asking about her, and I thought I should give it to you and you'd know what to do with it. I'll be away until Tuesday and will bring it by your office then."

He banged a fist on the table and tried calling the organ shop. Of course there was no answer. He sent Sarah an email back asking her to please call him any time, day or night, if she happened to check her email before Tuesday and got this message. Then he groaned when he saw another message in the queue that had appeared to come from himself. He reluctantly clicked on it.

Professor Gilpin's Means, Discourse, And Opportunity

The reiterative and citational practice by which discourse produces the effect that it names derives from the nonreductive distinction between *performance* on the one hand and *performativity* on the other. Yet the failure to make such distinction between "being" and "doing" is inherent in the discursive bias that informs the works of those who in the name of "clarity" and the privileging of "plain words" actually are the passive recipients of authority and consensus and who, with the false claim of "linguistic transparency," would silence those who aim to think the world more radically.

In other words: Isn't it funny that Professor Gilpin writes and talks about murders and then they happen?

By the way, think "anyone" else has noticed???!!

He tried to call Anika several more times. He called the hospital to find out about Wendy; she was still in serious condition. The rest of the time he sat at his desk, fiddling with his computer, checking his email over and over. Finally at nine o'clock a message from Anika arrived and he knocked over his lamp lunging at the mouse to click on it. "Please do not call or email me any more. It is strange you would speak of 'lies.' If you have the urge to tell the truth, I suggest you speak to the police. I also thought no one quoted from 'Kim' anymore because Kipling was considered a reactionary colonialist by postmodernist literary geniuses."

Ignoring her admonishment, he sent her a message back at once pleading for a chance to speak to her. He barely slept that night. Around three o'clock an odd, out-of-season thunderstorm swept through, setting the windowpanes rattling, sending the Scottie under the bed. Gilpin felt like crawling under there with him.

On Sunday there was a memorial service for Eric Travis. Ted arrived at Lawless Chapel a few minutes late, held up on the sidewalk on the way by a phalanx of students speaking on cell phones and walking slowly. Periodically the theme from a Budweiser commercial would electronically emanate from somewhere within the pack and one of the students would dig through her bag and pull out a phone and add another voice to the babel of competing conversation.

One of the girls had a cell phone in one hand and a shopping bag in the other and would occasionally spot a friend on the other side of the street and wave with her cell-phone-hand pinkie so she wouldn't have to take the phone away from her ear. Bits of her words drifted back more clearly than the others. "Where are you...well what kind of hang out was it?...you went ewwww?...oh, he went ewwww?...ewwwww."

Her words had imperceptibly begun to blend with a louder patter that was coming up from behind as a girl who had been following him drew closer. "Yeah...I'm walking on the sidewalk...no wait, so anyway last time we hung out he goes like ewwww no way and I'm like...no, he goes ewwwww...yeah, he goes like ewwwww no way, and I'm like well I didn't go ewwww when you wanted me to swallow it..."

He suddenly realized he'd been hearing two sides of the same conversation. He finally was able to take advantage of a break in the vehicular traffic to dart out into the road and get past the girls in front of him on the sidewalk.

In front of Lawless Chapel the storm had redistributed the leaves on the quadrangle that the grounds crews had spent the last week blowing into piles. He ducked into the side door of the chapel closest to Trojan Hall and found a seat near the front of the nave.

Looking around he saw Anika near the opposite end of a row a few behind him. She was sitting with Dr. John Doe and his wife, wearing a simple black knit dress that objectively would have been considered an appropriately somber sign of respect or mourning, but which had an effect on him of something like an electric shock to the groin. At that moment she caught his eye and quickly turned away.

The service was the standard academic formula, no hint of religious overtones disturbing the collection of mostly humorous reminiscences. The more of these things Gilpin went to, the more he felt there was something to be said for the reassuring formality of tradition; at weddings, too, but especially funerals. At least you knew how to act: the comfort of ancient liturgy, the steadying impersonality of the officiating clergyman, no embarrassing expectation of audience participation. But these days one never knew what to expect. He was amazed at the sang-froid of friends, husbands, wives, children, standing up at memorial services to read aloud pieces they had composed; but then there were the unpredictable times when someone lost it and broke down, or didn't know when to shut up, or told off-color jokes, or became so maudlin that the entire audience was reduced to staring awkwardly into their programs.

But Travis's friends pulled it off okay, with mostly gentle humor and a mostly restrained theatricality; only one speech that got lost in a clot of that kind of folksy erudition that academics seem to think makes them down-to-earth but whose actual effect is invariably the opposite: something about Eric as "the terpsichorean muse in the fabulous fandango that is life, ever ready to instruct those of us with two left feet in the choreography of the dance."

There was also usually a selection of favorite music: but Travis had had the same facetious general contempt for music that he had had for literature, and so his student who had played the organ concert the week before put together a few particularly campy nineteenth-century selections that probably would have appealed to Travis's sense of humor. There was a brilliantly allegro movement from one of the Mendelssohn sonatas, and Ted felt tears welling up in eyes at the arpeggiated major chords rippling forth in innocent joyous hopefulness, the mood only ruined by a typically Mendelssohnian over-the-top coda that went off the deep end into something that could have passed for Music for Space Shuttle Launch.

That had been followed by a final speech, by a friend of Travis's, who confined himself to a mere four sexual double entendres.

But the service had closed with a serious musical postlude, a piece Ted had never heard of before, a canonic etude by Schumann, the program said; it was a strict cannon at the unison in C major, clearly an homage to Bach, but with a Romantic soulfulness that moved him with its melancholy sense of straddling the centuries in a state of timeless suspension.

It was the perfect ending note, and for the few minutes the music had lasted he forgot his misery in a reverie about the finiteness of life, the immortality of great music, the works of man the only claim to the eternity of the soul.

He wandered out into the autumn afternoon and the bright sunshine and smell of leaves hit him a visceral force, sending his mood plummeting to where it had been. He suddenly couldn't bear the thought of catching another glimpse of Anika, and ducked into Trojan Hall.

The D-CADS corridor maintained its usual tomblike sense of desertion. Even Shalaby's office had the air of being unoccupied by human life. On an impulse he knocked softly on the door. The do not disturb sign hung in its usual place but no answer came from within. He knocked four more times. He listened for five minutes, then cautiously turned the knob. It was locked.

He opened his wallet and pulled out his university-issued American Express card and tried slipping it between the door and the frame. He had no idea what he was doing; he tried to remember how he had seen it done in movies. Nothing happened and he tried pushing harder.

The card snapped in half and one of the broken pieces rattled to the floor.

He'd always hated American Express, but he still looked around guiltily. He quickly shoved the pieces in his pocket and pulled out his thinner library card. This time he tried slipping it down from the top. Astonished, he found the door had silently swung open. He crept into the room, shutting the door softly behind.

As his eyes adjusted to the darkness that shrouded Shalaby's lair, they were drawn to the huge antitank dart sitting on the desk. He wondered if it really was toxic. Like a child who had just been told not to touch something, he found it irresistible, and picked it

up. It was surprisingly heavy for something so slender. He quickly
set it back down and found himself automatically wiping his hands
them on his pants, as if that would do any good.

He looked around Shalaby's desk. What the hell was he expecting to find—a confession signed in blood? A tell-tell hair left
by the murderer? A sprig of wild thyme that grew only in Julie
Glantz's yard?

He moved the desk chair out of the way and gingerly pulled
out the center drawer. It turned out to be just the keyboard tray
for the computer, but he saw a piece of white paper crammed in
at the back. He pulled farther. The drawer came out in his hands.
He tried to slide it back into the runners but the wheels kept re-
fusing to line up with the tracks. He started sweating.

He tried to put the entire drawer down on top of the desk; but,
as he raised it, the cables that ran from the keyboard and mouse
through a slot in the back of the drawer, under the desk, and then
around the front of the desk to the back of the computer jerked it
to a halt just short of the desktop. He tried tugging a bit more, and
the computer, pulled by the attached cables, lurched dangerously
toward the rear edge of the desk.

He stopped abruptly. He tried lowering the drawer to the floor
but the same thing happened. He tried balancing the drawer with
one hand, cradling it underneath, reaching behind the computer
on the desktop to unplug the keyboard cable, but found he
couldn't quite reach. He picked up the keyboard with one hand
while still balancing the drawer with the other but then the drawer
tipped sideways and the mouse slipped off the edge and was dangling by its wire; he hastily put the keyboard back down on the
drawer and retrieved the mouse, then managed to catch the
drawer at both ends just before it was about to tip over completely.

He looked at the office chair and again shifted the drawer to
one hand and stretched as far as he could with the other arm to
pull the chair over; he thought the cables would just reach to let
him put the drawer down on the chair arms. But the chair re-

mained a half inch out of reach. He stood there for a minute. He sat down on the floor, still holding the drawer in midair in front of the desk. He slowly tried to turn around. The short cables again halted him halfway around. He hunched down as low as he could, rested the drawer on his head and shifted his hands one at a time from the ends of the drawer to the front and back edges and then back to the ends as he slowly rotated his whole body 180 degrees around underneath, keeping the keyboard all the while in its same orientation to the desk.

He was now facing with the back of his head to the desk. He then slowly slid his legs out one at a time like a Russian dancer, then slid the rest of the way down, lowering his back flat on the floor, all the while keeping his head bent upright, the keyboard still resting on the top of his head and held on either end with his hands. He then started to try to hook the chair legs with his feet. And it was in this interesting position that Douad Shalaby found him when he chose that instant to walk into his office.

There was a moment of awkward silence. "Oh, hi Douad," Ted said, hoping against all odds that it sounded casual.

Shalaby said nothing, just glared menacingly.

"Um. You wouldn't be able to hold this drawer for a moment, would you? It just sort of slipped out."

Shalaby walked over and took it wordlessly. Ted got up. It was a measure of the moral depravity he felt that all he could think of was getting out of the situation with as few further words as possible. "Thanks. Well, I guess I'll see you later, Douad." As he hastily made for the door, he saw Shalaby trying to set the drawer down on top of his desk and pulling up short as the computer, dragged by the cables, hopped another inch toward the edge, then fell completely over, dragging in its wake a tangle of cables, and then, almost in slow motion, taking the monitor over the side with it, too. Ted didn't look back again, or break stride, until he was home and the door locked behind him.

✤ 17.

The student who appeared to be in charge of the demonstration that was taking place in front of Trojan Hall when Gilpin arrived on Monday afternoon carried a BlackBerry in one hand and a cell phone in the other. He was looking harried. Despite his retro sideburns and earring, he had the demeanor of a hyperorganized business executive.

"Well, where's the microphone?" he was saying into his phone. "I signed up with the Student Involvement Center for it. They were supposed to bring chalk, too. For the sidewalk chalking. What? Can you hold?...Hey—buddy. No, now they're saying you can only use chalk on the sidewalk in front of the Cuervo Center. Yeah, hold on, I'm on the other line with the guy now...Hello? Yeah, I don't think it's fair because they were counting on the chalking for their community service hours. Let me check." He poked at the BlackBerry and studied the result. "We've got the no tuition increase, the living wage for museum curators, the chicken boycott, the end grade discrimination, and...can you hold?..."

Gilpin made his way past the half dozen students holding signs. He felt a sudden black fury. Why didn't any of these little shits ever throw a brick through a window. Why didn't they write papers agonizing over the meaning of life. Why didn't they lose their hearts in hopeless loves that ended in wandering the streets at two a.m. and howling at the moon, instead of just "hooking up" and talking about it as if it was what TV show they had decided to watch the night before. Why didn't they get mad at someone and punch them in the nose. Hell, the only thing that ever got punched around here was their tickets on the good ship USS Meritocracy, sailing on the cruise to nowhere. The most challenging question he ever got in class these days was "is that going to be on the exam?"

Maybe he'd just flunk them all this term and see what happens. Give an A to the first one who said anything eccentric or offensive or unconventional.

He was still seeing black as he sat down at his desk and scanned the morning's crop of incoming emails. At the top was a message from the administrative offices of the university health services addressed to "the extended university health customer community":

> A security flaw in the university computer system was discovered over the weekend that may have made it possible under certain circumstances for university administrative personnel who are not members of the university health service administration to improperly access patient files.
>
> While we cannot find any evidence that any such improper accessing did occur, we cannot rule out the possibility.
>
> However, please be assured that any lapses that may or may not have occurred do not in any way alter our strong commitment to protecting patient privacy, as recently recognized by the university health services being ranked No. 1 among universities in Northern Ohio for its program to communicate to patients the 18 simple steps we each can take to help safeguard the security of our own medical records and for helping to develop and publicize the slogan, "Remember, 'Insecurity of patient medical records' always begins with 'I.'"

He furiously deleted the message, called the hospital for the ninth time to check on Wendy's condition, was told it remained serious, went to his bookshelf and pulled out a volume, and spent two hours reading Elizabethan love poems, hoping for the relief of a counter-irritant.

> *Love is a sour delight, a sug'red grief,*
> *A living death, an every-dying life,*
> *A breach of reason's law, a secret thief,*
> *A sea of tears, an everlasting strife ...*
>
> *What poor astronomers are they*
> *Take women's eyes for stars! . . .*
> *And love itself is but a jest*
> *Devis'd by idle heads*
> *To catch young fancies in the nest*
> *And lay them in fools' beds,*
> *That being hatch'd in beauty's eyes*
> *They may be fledg'd ere they be wise.*

God, he could put together a whole anthology—Renaissance Courtiers Kvetch About Women and Love.

> *Shall she never out of my mind?*
> *Nor shall I never out of this pain?*

At three-thirty Dr. Martin from the hospital phoned to say that he was informing everyone on the contact list that no one else had reported any symptoms since the dinner on Friday and that they were now focusing on a possible bacterial infection; Ms. Heatherton apparently had a rare immune system disorder that rendered her vulnerable. The culture should be back by tomorrow morning and they would know for sure. At three-fifty his phone rang; when he picked it up and he heard a click before he could even say hello. Oh God, not this again, he thought. But it didn't ring again.

A half hour later he heard a voice down the corridor. "Hey there, Doo-add, do you have a minute?" He recognized it, to his surprise, the confident tone of Bob Welch. "I've been wanting to sit down with some of our thought leaders..." The rest of his words faded away behind a closing door.

Five minutes later he heard a loud thump. It was about five minutes after that that he heard the door open and the voice ree-merge. "Well, really good to have this face time with you Doo-add," it was saying. "We've got a short time horizon, but we'll try to close the loop on this in the next week." He heard the door shut.

Several seconds later came a crashing sound. "Doo-add? Eve-rything okay in there?" Welch's voice was calling. Then came the sound of a door rattling and someone banging a few times, louder than just knocking.

A silvered head appeared in his doorway. "Ted—glad some-one's here. I think there's a problem with Doo-add. Can you give me a hand?" Ted quickly followed Welch back to Shalaby's door. "I was just in talking to him, but right after I left I heard a crash and he doesn't answer." Welch's corporate jargon had vanished, replaced by a tone of simple urgency. Welch called again through the door, then like a football tackle crashed his large entire frame against the door. He turned to Ted: "Does anyone have a key?"

"Yes, in the department office downstairs. I'll get it."

"I think he may have put the chain on the door right after I left," Welch said. As Ted ran for the stairs he heard Welch batter-ing against the door a few more times. Then came a splintering crash. Ted reversed direction and was back at Shalaby's doorway in fifteen seconds. The chain and the plate that had held it to the jamb were dangling from the door, still held in the keeper where it had been fastened to the door from the inside. Screw holes and splinters of wood marked where it had been ripped from the jamb when Welch had broken down the door.

Shalaby was on the floor behind his desk. Next to him was the antitank projectile, the gleaming metal of its point covered with bright red blood.

If it was true, as Raskolnikov said, that "man gets used to everything—the scoundrel," Gilpin had ample opportunities over the next three hours to feel grateful for the fact. Blood, policemen, and the monotony of giving the same answers over and over had all lost some of their novelty and saliency with repetition.

But the mind-numbing and anxiety-provoking tedium of waiting was one thing he thought he'd never get used to. After he had run through his story three times they had him sit in his office and wait—for what, was unclear—and the time crept by at a tortoise's pace. He felt almost grateful when the sergeant at last reappeared and asked him to tell him everything from the beginning once more.

"You're sure the door was locked, professor?" he asked when Ted was done.

"Yes—I mean Mr. Welch had to break it down. He must have tried five or six times before it gave way."

"You know, professor, one thing I give the U.S. Army. They sure know how to make a piece of metal that takes a beautiful fingerprint."

"You mean that thing—that was really what killed him?"

"Yup, that's what the doc says. Hit him right on the cranium."

"But how on earth..."

"I dunno. But facts are facts."

"You know, Professor Shalaby talked like thing was dangerous—I meant toxic. It's made of uranium or something. I mean I thought I ought to just mention it—you know, if your people are handling it they might want to be careful."

The cop looked as bored as always but got up wordlessly, sauntered off down the hall, and came back a minute later. "Doc says the only way that thing's toxic is if it knocks you on the cranium. That other stuff is a bunch of old wives' tales."

"Uh—oh. Okay. Look, you said something about fingerprints."

"Oh, yeah," he said as if an afterthought. "We got a beautiful set of yours on it."

"Oh." He felt his ears burning red. "Well I was in his office the other day and picked it up. Or tried to. It weighs a ton."

"Nine pounds. I wanted to ask you about that, professor, since you know we got a complaint from the deceased here about that. He said you had entered his office and were doing something with his computer when he found you that resulted in"—he looked at his notebook—"$2,569.42 in property damage."

"He filed a police report? Against me? For that?"

"Well, professor, maybe everybody is feeling a bit jumpy. But maybe you could tell me what this was all about. I mean in light of subsequent developments, it does take on a certain possible interest."

Gilpin winced. "Well, I just wanted to have a look around. His office was where that knife came from. And, well, dammit, you seem convinced that I'm somehow involved in all this, and my girlfriend's given me the heave-ho because *she* thinks I'm not telling the truth about it, and well, Christ, I just thought I had to do something to find out who's doing this and trying to make it look like I'm guilty. And they're doing a damn fine job of it, too. Bloody hell."

The cop let his eyes wander over Gilpin's bookshelves for a minute. "Professor, I did tell you that you ought to leave the detective business to the professionals, didn't I? You see, the way things are now, even if I want to assume the best, look where trying to do things yourself has got you. You break into the deceased's office, you put your fingerprints all over the death weapon. So, don't you think it's time you left things to us?"

Gilpin said nothing.

"Just of curiosity, though, professor," the cop said, still looking at the bookshelves, "this death have any resemblance to a mystery story, too?"

"Well, as a matter of fact it does." He spoke the words with the weary yet belligerent air of someone telling a truth he does not expect to be believed. "Another Sayers novel. *Busman's Honeymoon.* The victim is in a locked house. He's found dead from a blow to the head."

"And who did it in this one, professor?"

"The gardener. He rigs up a hanging cactus pot with extra weights and uses a piece of fishing line to hold it so it's pulled back, and when the victim opens the lid of his radio to listen to the news, which he does at the same time every night, the line is released and the plant swings and knocks him on the head."

The cop smiled a vague smile. "Sounds pretty elaborate, professor. And then, having the gardener do it breaks the rules, doesn't it?"

Gilpin did not reply. "Okey-dokey, professor. Never thought I'd have so much detective duty when I left homicide downtown for this job. But just take my advice, professor, please. For your own good. You want to become a policeman, go back to school, take classes on things like major issues in contemporary criminal justice, and learn to drink bad coffee and enjoy having deep conversations with drunks. You like what you're doing now better, then leave the police work to us."

It was another hour before the cops and technicians had cleared out of the building. Gilpin picked up the phone and called Mary and cursed when he got her answering machine. He peeked out into the corridor. Shalaby's door had three bands of yellow police tape across it. The building was dead quiet. The door gave way with a small amount of force. He bent and stepped through the police tape. With a deliberately contemptuous disdain for any remaining caution, he left the door wide open. To hell with it, he thought.

Just like in the movies, a chalk outline on the floor marked where the body had fallen. Behind the desk, running along the window, was a work table covered with stacks of papers. A hanging North African basket that Ted had not noticed before was suspended from the ceiling, low over the table. With his heart beating he stood up on the desk chair and examined the ceiling.

A small screw eye was twisted into the window frame behind the basket. Another larger screw eye was mounted into the ceiling directly over the desk.

He pulled the basket as far as it would go toward the wall and then let it swing free.

It swung in a low arc that came almost to the front edge of the work table, a few inches or so behind where Shalaby would have been sitting at his desk, his back to the window. He looked into the basket and pulled out a long piece of clear monofilament fishing line. It was attached to one of the cords that suspended the basket to the ceiling.

He threaded the line through the two screw eyes and saw it was just long enough to reach the edge of the keyboard tray on the desk when he pulled it as far as it would go, bringing the basket up against the wall. A small washer was tied on the end of the line. He closed the line into the front side edge of the tray, the washer catching it in the slot. When he pulled the tray out, the line flew free and the basket swung forward.

"Jesus Christ," he whispered to himself.

He was still staring at the swinging basket when he became aware of someone standing in the doorway. With a start he turned. It was Anika.

✢ 18.

She was looking at him with an expression he had never seen before on her face. Neither of them moved. "I'm sorry. I was wrong," she said simply. He remained frozen in the chair. She smiled wanly. "Generalizing from incomplete data. Classic error."

"But how..." he began.

"You mean you haven't figured it out? By now?"

He still was stuck in place. He finally managed to shake his head dumbly.

"But the email. Sorry I didn't look at it until just now. He was the only one who could have known, of course."

"I still don't know what you mean."

"The medical records. That Eric and Wendy had medical conditions that would make them susceptible." She saw he was still looking blank. "Oh, Ted, you are hopeless."

"I guess we knew that anyway."

"You see, it couldn't have been anyone but Welch."

"Welch?" He had never actually seen anyone's jaw drop, but he realized his had done that. "You're joking."

"I wish I were. Look, first he tried either to drive Julie to a breakdown with those messages, or maybe was hoping to just threaten her into cooperating with his plans. But then Eric figured out what was going on and tried to confront him. That was that note he had the copy of in his hand when you found him. Welch must have suggested a meeting at the organ chamber and locked him in, knowing it would kill him. At the same time, either because of dumb luck—or just plain dumbness on your part stumbling your way into this, Ted—he got the idea he could affix the blame on you by having all the murders copy murder mystery plots. I don't know whether he had that idea from the start or if it was only after Eric's death that he got the idea. But that's what happened. And you did a splendid job of falling into his plans."

"So the phone call on Monday..."

"Yes, that must have been him. First he made sure you were in your office, then after Mfuka was killed, he tricked you into blundering again onto the scene."

"And then Wendy—that was easy. Maybe he was just hoping the chocolates would kill everyone. God. Even you. And I was the perfect sap. Oh, God. He even convinced you. Didn't he."

"I'm sorry. It is embarrassing to make the same mistake I was accusing you of."

"But wait, Anika. Do you know what's happened? Except Welch couldn't have been involved."

He filled her in on what had taken place that afternoon. "And I was right here when he broke down the door. It had been chained from the inside. And look at what I've found." He showed her the mechanism to pull the hanging basket back and release it when the computer tray was pulled out of the desk. "So you see someone must have done this ahead of time. How could it have been Welch?"

She looked at the basket swinging. "Ted. You tried this?"

"Yes, I just showed you. And with that chunk of uranium in there it would have whacked him on the back of the head."

"And he was hit on the back of the head?"

"Yes, I saw the wound while he was lying on the floor."

"Ted, I don't suppose you happened to notice that if he was sitting in that chair facing his desk, the basket would not have swung far enough forward to reach the back of head."

"Well, yes, I saw that. But with that heavy weight in it, it would have."

She looked at him with the look one uses for a particularly large and not too bright dog that one is very fond of.

"I mean, right?" he said. "You have a heavy weight, it would swing faster. So it would go farther. I mean it stands to reason. Right?" He was growing less and less confident under her scornful expression.

"Ted. Did you truly never take any physics at all?"

"Well, not exactly physics. Not physics per se. Physics as such. Physics qua physics..."

"Okay. A pendulum. It cannot swing to a farther angle forward than the angle it starts from back. It doesn't make any difference how much weight there is. Don't you know the acceleration of any object by gravity is independent of its mass?"

"Uh. Well, not exactly. I mean if you put it that way..."

"Okay. F equals ma. You know that, surely. Newton's second law. And because the force of gravity is mg, the m's cancel out. Oh, God, Ted, tell me you're joking. You really do not know this? This is baby level. This is like someone not knowing what a noun or a verb is. I cannot believe they let people out into the world with such ignorance. Unless there was some way to start with this pendulum on the other side of that back wall, it could not swing far enough forward to hit someone on the head over here if it had a ten ton weight on it."

"Oh."

"So this whole thing was set up again afterward to make it look like good old Professor of Literature Ted Gilpin had been reading too many Dorothy Sayers novels for his own good. By someone else who perhaps was a physics ignoramus, I might add. He was probably counting on you to bumble your way in and 'discover' it yourself, which of course is even better."

"Yes. I guess I've been an expert at that," he glumly agreed. "But look, Anika, how does this solve the problem. The door was still locked from the inside."

She paused for several seconds, obviously mulling it over.

"Tell me again the sounds you heard. I mean before Welch came to you to ask for help."

"Well, there was a thump. Like someone knocking something over. A dull sound. Then about five minutes later there was something that sounded like maybe something breaking. Or a door crashing. That's when Welch appeared and asked me to help."

"Well, suppose he had already killed him with the big dart."

"But how could he have done that. Douad was hit on the back of the head. And he was facing the door at the time."

"No, we do not know that at all. You are just assuming he was because of your crazy plant idea. Maybe he turned around and was struck on the back of the head by someone who was standing here in front of the desk and picked up this thing when he saw his chance. One quick strike would have done it by your description of it. Then he fixed up this plant apparatus. Then he goes to the door, puts the chain on, and pulls it very hard open from the inside breaking the chain off the wall. That was the crash you heard. Then he closed the door and made sure he had you here while he pretended to break down the door from the outside so he would have a witness to its supposedly being fastened on the chain. And you weren't right there at the exact instant he got the door open, were you, so you couldn't exactly see what happened?"

"Jesus."

They looked at each other for a minute. "But look, can this guy be that smart?" Ted asked suddenly. "I mean this is like Professor Moriarty to come up with all this stuff."

"Who is this. Some other postmodern literary genius?"

"Uh, no. He's the evil character in Sherlock Holmes. Christ, Anika, how can you be so smart about all this and never have even read Sherlock Holmes. You do know who Sherlock Holmes is?"

"Yes, I have heard of Sherlock Holmes. And it is probably because I have never filled my mind with all of these stories, and with your ideas about narrative and text, that I am good at it. And I know something about the laws of the universe. Which you might think would be relevant to anyone who wants to understand the things that go on in it."

"Well, look my point is Welch is just some business-cliché spouting jock who spent his entire adult life selling sugary pieces of cardboard to toddlers. And college students," he added, remembering the sight he had often seen in the dining hall of students filling up huge bowls of Lucky Charms for lunch and dinner. He looked at his watch. "Look, maybe we're both nuts. Maybe we'd better sleep on this. I mean for God's sake we can't go to the police making an accusation like this unless we're absolutely sure about it. And when it gets right down to it, what proof do we have. I'm just—well, glad you know it wasn't me. You don't what kind of hell I've been through the last few days."

"I think I have an idea. Since I was going through something worse."

"Oh—right. Typical self-centered moron, sorry. I hadn't thought of that."

"Well, let's go."

"What do you mean?"

"You said, let's sleep on it. You wouldn't want me to do that by myself, would you?"

They went.

The next morning they were sitting side by side in front of the pocked metal desk in the police sergeant's office. The sergeant was on the other side of the desk, leaning all the way back in an old office swivel chair, his hands over his belly, a look of supremely tolerant skepticism on his wide face. He had listened to Gilpin without saying a word, only glancing at Anika from time to time.

When Ted had finished he sat there nodding his head a few times, scratched behind his ear, and slowly let his chair return to an upright position.

"Professor," he began, "you know, I think maybe we've all been reading too much into things."

He opened a folder on his desk, extracted a sheet of paper, and tossed it across the desk to Gilpin. "That's the medical report on Professor Heatherton. Salmonella. Apparently she has a condition that makes her susceptible. That's why she's the only one who got sick."

Gilpin read the page, full of medical terminology—patient reports known history of interferon-gamma receptor deficiency—positive obtained from sample of chocolates on immunoenzymatic LPS plate test—prognosis guarded.

"Whoever heard of salmonella showing up in chocolates?" Gilpin said. "I mean accidentally?"

"Apparently it's happened, professor. The doctor said he checked with the public health people. There was a case in Canada a couple of years ago. Belgian chocolates—exact same brand."

Anika spoke up, her clear quiet voice cutting through the bad country music that drifted in from somewhere down the corridor. "But, sergeant, surely it cannot be another coincidence. Here is a second case where if someone had access to faculty medical records, they could carry out a murder, or attempted murder in this case—at least we still hope it is only attempted murder in the case of Wendy Heatherton—and make it look like an accident or natural causes."

"And I checked with the student who supposedly gave me the chocolates," Gilpin chimed in. "She says she didn't give me any chocolates or anything else."

The sergeant raised his eyes. "Professor, these kids change their stories as often as they change their socks. Which means every three days. So, she got worried. She got embarrassed. How the hell do I know? What's more likely to you. A student buys a bunch of crappy candy and gets scared and says she didn't give 'em to you when someone lands in the hospital afterward? Or a university vice president goes around putting salmonella in boxes of chocolates and knocking off faculty members he doesn't like? I mean, come on, professor."

"But I've shown you the motive. Every single one of the victims is someone who stood in the way of his plans. He had to get rid of us or his whole business plan would be a failure."

The sergeant uncharacteristically winced. "Professor, you know, I remember reading somewhere about how academic politics are so nasty because the stakes are so small. But somehow I don't think even something this small would drive someone to start committing murders left and right."

"What about what you were saying to me last week yourself? About all these clues? About things being so elaborate and complicated, like someone was deliberately trying to lay false trails? I mean, and how could these things happen to so exactly follow the plots of mystery novels if someone wasn't doing it deliberately?"

"Well, professor, I think maybe I've been hanging around a university too long myself." He chewed his cheek meditatively. "But you know, it kinda occurred to me that I was getting too fancy for my own good. In fact, I was making the exact same mistake that that guy Bayard was pointing out, which is a bit ironic if you think about it. You get sold on an idea, you can always find clues to support it. There's only so many ways a person can get themselves killed, when it gets right down to it. So you start with the idea people are getting themselves killed the same way as a bunch of mystery stories, sure you're going to find similarities if you look for them. I bet every death in the coroner's files have something about them that might remind you of some famous mystery story. So what. That's life."

"What about the others? Travis? And Bariki? And Shalaby?"

The sergeant opened another folder. He put on his glasses and shuffled through the papers. "M.E. says Travis died of cardiac arrest induced by severe stress, exacerbated by underlying condition of aortic valvular stenosis. No evidence of foul play. Bariki. Ruled as suicide. Shalaby. Accidental death."

"*Accident?* How could he accidentally run a metal spike through his head?"

"Apparently he did really have the thing hanging up over his table, that much was like you said. To show it off, like some kid with a model airplane. Hell, I guess kids don't play with model airplanes anymore, but it's what we used to do. Hang it on a string. So he's leaning way over the table, maybe to open the window, and he raises his head up fast and, bam, knocks that point into his cranium. He apparently likes to keep it dark in there while he's working, so he wouldn't have seen it."

Ted shook his head incredulously. "But then what about this thing rigged to make it look like the murder device in *Busman's Honeymoon?*"

The cop looked like someone had asked him what he thought of ancient fertility rites in lower Borneo. "Professor, you walk into any office here there's things screwed into the ceiling to hold plants and stuff. Now you look at this stuff, and you think of some elaborate detective story plot you read. Anybody else looks at it and thinks of hanging plant holders. And you yourself just told me anyway that the thing couldn't have worked to kill him while he's sitting at his desk. So, aren't we back where we started?"

"And Bariki—suicide? I can't imagine Bariki had a reason on earth to kill himself. And especially in such a gruesome way."

"Well, professor I'm told he was upset about the university dog policy."

"What? You're saying he killed himself because he couldn't bring his dog to the office anymore?"

"There's also the impostor syndrome," the sergeant said, knowingly.

"And what is that supposed to be?" said Anika.

"Well, professor," the cop said, turning to Anika, "I'm no psychologist but it's important to be up on psychology in our work. Apparently it's not uncommon among intellectuals and academics. Especially your women, your African-Americans." He pulled out a large textbook, opened it to a page marked with a post-it note, and read. "'An internal experience of intellectual fraudulence, particularly among high-achievers. The belief that one is not deserving of his/her career success. An intense subjective fear of the inability to repeat past success.'"

"Sergeant, for God's sake, can't you see this," Gilpin erupted. "I mean the whole picture? How can you sit there and let this, well, madman just get away with it? And then there's still Julie Glantz. What if she's been killed too."

"Yeah, except she hasn't."

"What do you mean?"

"We found her, professor. Didn't anyone tell you? She's at a monastery in New Mexico. Meditating, she says. Apparently the pressures of her life got to be too much for her. And then those prank messages pushed her over the edge a bit. She's fine. Just one of those things that happens to high-strung academic types. We've seen it before."

The three of them sat wordlessly for a minute. The sergeant broke the silence. "Look, professor, I've got to deal with facts and we haven't got any facts beyond what I've shown you. We've had a string of tragedies. That's all. If you think I'm going to arrest a vice president of the university I work for on a triple murder charge based on a literary theory that a professor and his nice girlfriend have cooked up, you're wrong. You know, you've come up with a real clever story that connects all the dots. Why don't you turn it into a detective novel. Maybe you can make some money on it. But I've got work to do, professor."

"No, sergeant, I don't think it would make a good detective novel at all. It breaks just about every one of the rules, remember? The rules say no hidden clues, no multiple detectives, and the culprit has to be brought to justice in the end."

"Yeah, I remember. And no love interest, either," he said, grinning at Anika. She didn't return his smile.

"Well, we'll just have to find the proof, that's all," Gilpin said. "Thanks sergeant. You'll see we were right."

✛ 19.

Ted and Anika walked back across the quadrangle in silence.
The leaf blower brigade was at work again. This time they were
wearing dark blue windbreakers, which were emblazoned with
"The College Of . . ." on the front and " . . . VISA" on the back.
"Ted," she finally said, straining to be heard over the noise. "I
keep thinking that you are the only one left. And if Welch has
failed to pin the blame on you, then you may be in danger."

"No, I don't think so. He's got what he's wanted. We can't
prove a thing. He knows it. He's won already."

"Well, be careful." As they parted he found himself definitely
on the receiving end of a shockingly passionate kiss. "See you tonight," she said, then turned for the door of the science building.

"Anika!" he called after her.

She turned back. "Look, I have to ask you this—even though I
know it breaks all the rules. But I've just got to know. What was it
that first attracted you to me? Was it when I played 'Waiting at
the End of the Road' on the piano at the party?"

She laughed, astonished and incredulous. "What on earth
made you think that?"

"Oh, I don't know. So what was it?"

"Your furry eyebrows."

"Okay, ask a stupid question."

"What makes you think there's a reason? That's very linear
and rational of you." She shook her head. "Bye," she said with a
sort of schoolteacher firmness, and this time turned and didn't

look back. Gilpin made his way up to his office. He turned on his computer, and on a sudden impulse clicked on the music player and found "Heart and Soul." Corny song, the one everyone always banged out in terrible piano duets when he was a kid, but magic in Connee Boswell's hands, her sensuous voice melting each phrase.

> *Heart and soul*
> *I fell in love with you*
> *Heart and soul*
> *The way a fool would do—*
> *Madly*
> *Because you held me tight*
> *And stole a kiss in the night*

At the top of his email inbox was a message with the subject line, "TCO exec lauded for 'giving something back.'" He clicked on it, and read the press release from the university communications office with vacant astonishment:

> Saying that serving his alma mater "has been a dream come true," Robert Welch today informed the TCO Board of Trustees that he will be resigning his position as Vice President effective immediately.
>
> "It has been my lifelong aspiration to give something back," Welch said. "I am proud of being able to serve this world-class university. But it is time to move on to new opportunities." Chambers Brunswick Newton, President of The College Of, expressed his deep appreciation today for the business initiatives Welch had instituted in the management reform and academic growth of the university.
>
> "Bob is a true visionary leader, and we are deeply grateful to his model of selfless service," said Newton. "We wish him well in his new endeavors."

Welch, 54, will immediately assume the position of pro-vice chancellor of the University of the South Pacific in Fiji, and will also serve as director of the University's Center for the Study of Offshore Banking. "Bob's expertise as a business leader and academic innovator were an irresistible combination," said Taufe'ulungaki Malielegaoi, Chancellor of University of South Pacific. "TCO's loss is USP's gain."

Ted immediately clicked onto the student newspaper website, which always could be counted on to have the real story. legal woes squeeze juice read the lead headline. The story below it began:

Calling it a scandal 'second only to Enron,' prosecutors sought to question former Lawless Veep Bob 'Juice' Welch yesterday about his dealings at General Cereal, where he apparently was the key figure in a complex scheme to defraud investors by launching subsidiary shell companies which invested in commodity futures.

But Welch had left town only hours earlier. University officials confirmed late last night he had resigned his post as vice president and would announce today that he was taking a position in Fiji, which does not have an active extradition treaty with the United States.

A former co-worker of Welch's at General Cereal, who spoke on condition of anonymity, said, 'He put on this act of being just this dumb football player, but he was a master of the game. You know, the smartest guy in the room. And someone else's fingerprints were always the only ones you could find on everything he touched.'"...

Ted was still reading, transfixed, when there came a gentle knock on the door. He turned around and saw Sarah from the organ curator's shop standing in the doorway with a brown paper parcel, tied in string, in her hands. "Hi. Sorry we kept missing each other," she said. "Here's the package. I figured you'd know better what to do with it than me."

Ted leapt up with an alacrity that made her physically start. "Oh, sorry," he said. "Thanks." He almost grabbed the parcel out of her hands and began feverishly pulling the strings off and tearing off the paper. She stared in amazement. "Uh, okay," she said. "Well, I'll leave you to it, then. See you."

Ted made an inarticulate reply and continued pulling the paper off. Inside was an ordinary, red three-ring binder. He took it to the desk and sat down, his hands literally shaking. The cover of the first page bore the title GREAT JEWISH FOXHUNTERS.

The entire manuscript that followed was seven pages long. There were four pages on Siegfried Sassoon, who, the second paragraph noted, technically wasn't Jewish because his mother was not Jewish. There were two pages on a British Army officer of the nineteenth century who had traveled to Palestine, gone native by converting to orthodox Judaism, and continued foxhunting after his return to England. The seventh page was titled "Marvin Glantz," but was otherwise blank. That was it.

He picked up the binder to look at the back cover, but as he did so a photograph and letter in an envelope that had been loosely placed in it fell out.

The photograph was of a large man seated on a powerful-looking bay horse. He wore a bright red coat, a black top hat, and shiny black boots with brown leather tops. A pack of hounds was gathered around him. Written in ink at the bottom of the photo was "Marvin Glantz, Master of Foxhounds, Xenia Hunt, 1976." Though lacking the full bloodhound-like jowls, there was no mistaking the face of the man in the photograph. The Master of Foxhounds of the Xenia Hunt was, beyond any shadow of a doubt, a younger, one-hundred-fifty-pounds lighter, version of 'G.' himself.

He opened the envelope and removed the letter. It was addressed to "My dear Julie," and dated September of that year.

My dear Julie,

To say that I was surprised to receive your letter would be an understatement. To a man of my generation, poverty was the great shame. Perhaps even the one great shame. I could readily understand a child being ashamed of parents who had nothing. I could never understand the perversity, however, of a child feeling shame at parents who had everything; parents who indeed could and did provide their child everything she wished.

But there are many things in this world I no longer comprehend, and the resentment of one's children surely ranks high among those things. So I had largely reconciled myself to your determination to deny your family history and fortune. I say nothing of the heartbreak at your determination never to bear a child and provide your father a grandchild.

Thus your sudden application for such a considerable sum of money seemed—forgive me, hypocritical—to say the least. But I am willing to give you what you ask if you will do something for me in turn.

As you well know, it has always been my fondest desire to have my accomplishments in the hunt field and my singular stature as MFH of the Xenia Hounds be immortalized in, yes, print. To a man of my heritage there is something still sacred—foolish you no doubt think, but there it is—about the printed word. If you will write the book I spoke of to you these many years ago I will give you the money. It is as simple as that.

If you wish to keep your role a secret, I will respect your wishes, and will communicate with you in the future disguising my own name. I am sure a scholar of your resources can find a sufficient number of other great foxhunters among my co-religionists to make a manuscript of sufficient weight to justify publication in book form. I will of course arrange for the actual publication myself. All you need do is supply the text.

Your still loving father,
Marvin Glantz

He typed "Marvin Glantz" into Google and immediately found a website for Glantz Faucets in Xenia.

He dialed the telephone number. "Please listen carefully, as our menu has recently changed," a nauseously cheery recorded female voice answered. Three minutes later he was still pushing buttons, until he finally got the heavily Indian accented voice of a live human being on the line.

"Helllo, my name is Frrred. How may I help you?" He luxuriously rolled his "l" and "r."

"Could I speak to Mr. Glantz?"

"Whom may I tell him is calling, please?"

"Professor Ted Gilpin."

"And how is everything where you are, today, Professor Gilpin?" asked the Indian voice.

"Fine, fine."

"And Notre Dame played a very, very exciting game, yes, this weekend, did they not?"

"Uh, well, I'm not much of a sports fan."

"Ah, well the weather here in Ohio is very good today, I said to myself when I woke up this morning and looked out of my window. Such a pleasant fall day here in Ohio, America."

"Right. Umm, you know it actually doesn't bother me if you're really in Bangalore, but could I please speak to Mr. Glantz?"

"Marvin Glantz's office," another voice finally answered. Ted again identified himself. "I'll see if Mr. Glantz is available, sir. Will he know what this is in regards to?"

"Yes. Yes, I believe he will."

At last a familiar baritone voice came on the line. "Marvin Glantz speaking."

"Oh, hello. This is Ted Gilpin, Mr. Glantz. Or maybe I should say, 'G.'"

There was a small chuckle from the other end of the wire. "Ah, Professor Gilpin, I see you are a man of resources. Penetration. I suppose I should have known you could not solve the one mystery without solving the ancillary mystery. Very well. I am in your hands. I understand my daughter has been traced to New Mexico and is alive and well. But tell me—no more beating around the bush—have you got it?"

"Yes, Mr. Glantz. I do. But look, I think you're going to be disappointed. It's only seven pages. Apparently she never could find more than two other great Jewish foxhunters. And none of them is even really Jewish. Besides you, I mean."

"I see." His voice was neutral and controlled.

"I'll be honest with you," Gilpin continued with unaccustomed boldness. "I think it was mortifying enough for her to sell her scholarly integrity for this strange, well, vanity project, in the first place. And then to find she couldn't even get it done must have been unbearable. And the constant threat she was going to be exposed. First from Welch, who obviously had found out about it and was blackmailing her to go along with his plans. And then from Wendy Heatherton. No wonder she cracked under the strain. I'm not sure you did her any favor."

"I see," he repeated. "Professor Gilpin, you may judge me a hard man, and I will not deny your judgment. I meant well. Yet it is one of the perversities of this world that deeds of philanthropy have a way of never turning out as one expects. I have been a very generous man with the fortune I have accumulated as a pioneering manufacturer in the high-end luxury faucet industry, but I was doomed to bitter disappointment over the effects of my generosity. I see am fated to be disappointed again."

Ted said nothing, and Glantz continued in his tone of wistful, if orotund, detachment. "Yes, I gave away very considerable sums—much to your very university, in fact. Anonymously. Endowing professorships, scholarships. A new dormitory, even. Oh, yes. Your president convinced me I would be helping other youths, such as I was myself once, who lack the advantages of wealth and family. In that, alas, I was completely mistaken."

"Look, Mr. Glantz, you really don't have to tell me this. I feel like I've been prying into other people's business too much lately as it is."

"No, Professor Gilpin, please indulge me. It would do me good to get this off my chest. And perhaps from this—we may call it a parable—you will understand my actions toward my daughter—your colleague—better."

He cleared his throat melodramatically.

"Yes, I bestowed this considerable sum of money on your university. In the furtherance of lofty—and, if you will permit me to use such a term—noble purposes, as I conceived them. Advancing scholarship. Providing opportunity to the disadvantaged. Extending the benefits of education. You may think me naïve, or perhaps just innocent. But in my innocence I truly believed universities to be the last bastion of culture, the final firebreak against the all-consuming inferno of crudity and ignorance that threatens our latter-day civilization. 'A place of light, of liberty, and of learning,' as the great Benjamin Disraeli put it.

"Yes, Professor Gilpin, I thought the pursuit of scholarship was the last arena in which the values of selflessness, truth, and love of knowledge for its own sake still might hold at bay the rampant commercialism that now besets our every waking hour, heartlessly prizing the quarterly bottom line over the struggles of a lifetime—yea, a millennium. I thought that the universal patrimony of art and science that is the heritage of our great Western civilization was the irrefutable answer to the narrow tribalism of class, and the befogging superstition of religion, that have strangely reinfected this land once known for its devotion to equality and practical know-how. I thought that educational opportunity would erase the remaining boundaries of inherited advantage in our—supposedly—democratic society.

"Alas, Professor Gilpin, the more I gave, the more I learned how wrong I was, on every count. The famous professors hired to fill these endowed chairs turned out to care less about the selfless addition to the body of shared human knowledge than they cared for public celebrity and its attendant advantages of fame, wealth, and personal sexual gratification. The students, far from having their minds broadened, and learning to question themselves, merely acquired a smattering of facts and a patina of glib erudition, the better to inflict their undisturbed ignorance and self-satisfaction upon the world.

"And far from seeking to extend opportunity, the university administration, I discovered, was at heart interested only in serving affluent parents with a well-oiled achievement machine designed to confer the imprimatur of success upon the already successful.

"Oh, your university makes an ostentatious show of subsidizing the full costs for those students from the lower income brackets. But it has little to lose from so grand a gesture, since your admission procedures guarantee that no more than a few percent of students ever come from such a lowly station. Far more profitable, from the university's perspective, to use scholarship funds to reward those students who need it the least—those robotic products of test-preparation courses and summer enrichment camps and college consultants so devoutly patronized by their achievement-oriented parents who have already secured a place among the affluent and educated classes.

"A pact of the devil, Professor Gilpin. You give us your perfect 800's on the SAT tests, we give you a 'free ride' to boost our rankings in the *U.S. News* surveys. 'Dialing toll free' I believe is the amusing term students apply to this phenomenon, in which full scholarships are awarded to those with a perfect 800 score on the

SAT examinations, in spite of their invariably having no monetary need whatever for such assistance. No, Professor Gilpin, no institution in our society has better mastered the art of taking from the rich to give to the rich."

His voice began to take on a sentimental quaver as he moved into what was clearly the peroration of his speech.

"No, to truly make a commitment to the education of the underprivileged, a university such as yours would have to insist—actually insist—that its teachers teach—something that neither its overprivileged faculty, nor the legions of precociously practiced young meritocrats who arrive each year, having already spent their entire formative years jumping through the hoops of achievement, have the least interest in.

"To the underprivileged, college is the greatest opportunity in their life. To most of *your* students, it is merely another predetermined step on the escalator of success that their parents have provided them since infancy without question. The exclusive preschools, the private soccer coaches, the ballet lessons, the internships at law firms, the two weeks in Peru building houses for the worthy poor. And so naturally they expect to be rewarded with As for simply being there; and so they would bitterly resent being challenged actually to use their minds in class.

"So you see, Professor Gilpin, a long-winded way of saying, I am a man used to disappointment."

"I'm sorry.... But you know, this book idea. Honestly, it was crazy."

"Yes, I know that now. But I thought perhaps it might bring my daughter closer to me. I was mistaken about that as well."

"I'm sorry. I—Well, happy hunting, sir."

"Thank you. Goodbye, Professor Gilpin. If nothing else, it was an honor making your acquaintance. Perhaps we could meet and discuss literature some time. You see, I still have a naïve admiration for the pursuit of scholarship in spite of it all. Goodbye."

Gilpin sat quietly, meditatively for a moment.

Then he picked up the phone and dialed.

"Hello, mom?"

"Oh, Theodore. Such a surprise. What's wrong?"

"Nothing's wrong."

"You're sure nothing's wrong?"

"Yes, of course I'm sure."

"I just thought, you wouldn't be calling unless something was wrong."

"Mom. Nothing's wrong."

"I know it's crazy, but the first thing I thought when I heard your voice, was maybe it was bad news about your colonoscopy."

"Mom. I haven't had a colonoscopy."

"Well, you should. They had it on the *Today* show."

"Mom. Just listen to me. All I was calling to say is that I'm coming for Thanksgiving. And I'm bringing Anika with me."

"Anika? What kind of name is that. Is that a girl?"

"Yes, of course, mom. It's the woman I've been telling you about."

"Telling me? You never tell me anything. But, okay, so a mother is the last to hear. So, I'm very happy. Is she a vegetarian? I know a lot of these girls are these days."

"No, mom. No, definitely not."

"Okay, so good thing I ordered the thirty-four pound turkey. Now, Theodore. I was just reading in the *New York Post* where all these crazy professors are taking over the colleges these days. And all they do is say bad things about the other professors. It said, in this article, it's like a jungle there on college campuses. The politics. The fighting. The back stabbing. Oy, it was like a Stephen King novel. So, all I'm saying is, you should be careful."

He paused. "Okay, mom. I will."